MAYA
AND THE
THE RISING DARK

MAYA AND THE RISING DARK

BY

RENA BARRON

HOUGHTON MIFFLIN HARCOURT
BOSTON NEW YORK

hmhbooks.com

The text was set in Adobe Garamond Pro.

Library of Congress Cataloging-in-Publication Data
Names: Barron, Rena, author.
Title: Maya and the rising dark / by Rena Barron.
Description: Boston : Houghton Mifflin Harcourt, [2020] | Summary: "A
twelve-year-old girl discovers her father is the keeper of the gateway
between our world and The Dark, and when he goes missing
she'll need to unlock her own powers and fight a horde of
spooky creatures set on starting a war"—Provided by publisher.
Identifiers: LCCN 2019020312 (print) | LCCN 2019022285 (ebook) |
ISBN 9781328635181 (hardcover) | ISBN 9780358106227 (ebook)
Subjects: CYAC: Magic—Fiction. | Missing persons—Fiction. |
African Americans—Fiction. | Fantasy.
Classification: LCC PZ7.1.B37268 May 2020 (print) |
LCC PZ7.1.B37268 (ebook) | DDC [Fic]—dc23
LC record available at https://lccn.loc.gov/2019020312
LC ebook record available at https://lccn.loc.gov/2019022285

Manufactured in the United States of America
DOC 10 9 8 7 6 5 4 3 2
4500810295

For all the people like me who feel stuck between . . .
and for my family

ONE

THE DAY COLOR BLED FROM THE WORLD

T-MINUS FIVE DAYS.

Five long and torturous days until school was out for the summer. Not a moment too soon either. My math teacher, Ms. Vanderbilt, kept me in after-school tutoring the whole year. She said I was *gifted*, but to be honest, I had no clue what she was talking about half the time. My brain felt as lumpy as the vanilla pudding they served in the cafeteria on Mondays.

"Practice makes perfect, Maya," Ms. Vanderbilt chimed at her desk. "Get to work."

"Yes, ma'am," I mumbled back as I stared at the chalkboard.

Only the top of her red 'fro poked out from behind the tower of papers. If she didn't give so many quizzes, she wouldn't have a stack of tests to grade that stretched from Chicago to LA.

Today she had me working on *situational* math, and my head hurt just thinking about all the steps needed to solve the problem. She had written a recipe for candy apples and the price of the ingredients. Apples, Popsicle sticks, sugar, food coloring, corn syrup. I had to figure out how much it would cost to make fifty candy apples. This *wasn't* really rocket science, but math took time and focus, both of which I was short on.

Ms. Vanderbilt got worked up about fractions and decimals the way my friend Frankie got excited about science projects. Now, Frankie, she was a genius. She had the grades and IQ to prove it. But to me, math was about as interesting as watching paint dry, which was actually a thing I had to do for art class once.

I glanced over my shoulder at the clock on the wall.

Fifteen more minutes, then *goodbye, school—hello, weekend.*

Papa was due back from his work trip. I bit my lip, wondering what he'd bring me this time. My favorite gift was the red-and-gold sash he swore belonged to the great orisha Oya from my favorite comic book.

Oya wasn't real. So, of course, the sash wasn't really hers. Still, it was pretty, and I wore it to school for a week straight.

I dragged the chalk across the board, taking my sweet time. No way was I squeezing in another math problem before four o'clock. As long as Ms. Vanderbilt heard the *sound* of writing, she would keep her attention on grading papers and not on me.

As I worked out the cost of one candy apple, a shadow fell outside the window. I was trying to concentrate, but something edged at the back of my mind. It was the same feeling I had in gym class the other day when we were stretching on our mats after track. I spotted something wrong with the ceiling—like it was splitting open. But when I blinked, it was gone.

My gaze slid to the window, and my eyes slipped out of focus. My vision faded in and out. The world pulsed like a heartbeat, getting bigger, then smaller, then bigger again. The birds in the oak tree stopped chirping. I couldn't even hear the hum of cars on the streets anymore. The sound of the ticking clock on the wall vibrated in my ears. Seconds stretched into minutes.

My anemia made me dizzy sometimes, but it usually didn't last long. I leaned my shoulder against the wall next to the chalkboard and squeezed my eyes shut, waiting for it to pass. At least it wasn't happening in the middle of something important again. Last week my team lost the kickball tournament when my anemia struck. Most of the kids didn't blame me, but I still felt horrible.

When the dizziness went away, I opened my eyes again and my jaw dropped. I couldn't believe what I was seeing. The color bled from the world like someone was sucking it away through a straw. The window was gray. So were the trees, the sky, and the school flag. At first, I thought the sun hid behind the clouds, but this was something else. Something was wrong. Black lightning etched across the sky like ripples moving on the surface of a lake.

I snapped my head around to look at Ms. Vanderbilt, my heart thundering against my chest. She was still hunched over her papers, but she was *frozen*. Not frozen like a Popsicle, but frozen as if time had stopped. I wiped my sweaty hands on my pants. Frankie would say there has to be a reasonable explanation, but nope, there was nothing reasonable about this. This was bad, *really* bad.

"Ms. Vanderbilt?" I said, my voice shaking.

When she didn't answer, I blinked twice, unable to think. Then as if someone waved their wand and put everything right, the leaves on the tree changed from ash gray to dull yellow to green. Birdsong poured into the classroom again. Cars droned on the streets. Voices drifted in from the hall.

"My goodness, Maya," Ms. Vanderbilt said suddenly. "I didn't mean to keep you late."

I jumped so hard that the chalk fell from my hand and cracked in two on the floor.

Leaning around her papers, my math teacher frowned

at me. By the puzzled look on her face, Ms. Vanderbilt hadn't seen the bleeding gray or the black lightning. She'd been in some kind of trance the whole time. If I told her what happened, she'd laugh and say that I had a vivid imagination. I stared up at the clock again. It was now four fifteen. Thirty minutes had passed in what felt like seconds. Maybe I was daydreaming and it *was* my imagination.

I pressed my lips together, deciding to keep my mouth shut.

A crash rang in the hallway, and both Ms. Vanderbilt and I turned to the door. My friend Eli pressed his face against the glass, his fist ready to knock again. He smiled, his freckles standing out against his light brown skin. Ms. Vanderbilt shook her head at him.

Before she could dismiss me, I shrugged into my coat and threw my backpack across my shoulder. My math teacher squinted at my unfinished work. "We'll continue Monday."

"Yes, Ms. Vanderbilt," I grumbled, and jetted into the hallway, where Eli was playing with his phone. A few other kids were in the hall too, coming from extracurricular activities or tutoring or, like Eli, detention. He had a knack for getting in trouble.

This morning he put a frog in our English teacher's desk because she gave him a C-minus on his paper about famous ghosts. She couldn't prove Eli did it, but he doubled over laughing when she screamed. So he got detention for that.

Eli glanced up from his phone and frowned. "Was tutoring that bad?"

I sucked in a deep breath. "I'll tell you later."

Once outside, Eli and I stood with a group of kids waiting to cross the street. But Zane, the crossing guard, and his bloodhound weren't directing traffic. Instead, he was talking to Principal Ollie, whose gray suit and yellow tie were impeccable. Some parents had trouble remembering Principal Ollie's pronouns were *they* and *them*, not *him* or *her*. But everyone I knew got it.

"What's his malfunction?" an eighth grader whispered to his friend.

I couldn't tell if he meant Zane or his dog, General, who was howling at the sky. The crossing guard's hands curled into fists at his sides as he said something too low to hear. I wondered — no I hoped — he'd seen something too. No way was I the only one who saw the world turn gray. If he'd seen something, then that meant I really hadn't lost my mind. Principal Ollie patted Zane on the shoulder, and he winced and waved for us to cross. The hound stopped howling and wagged his tail.

On the way home, I broke down and told Eli every-thing. He bounced on his toes the whole time and asked me so many questions that my head spun again.

"Did you feel a cold spot?" Eli asked. "Like when there's a ghost around."

I shook my head at his latest question. "I can't remember."

"Did you sense a new *presence* in the room?"

We cut across a vacant lot covered in trampled weeds between two buildings. Some kids from Jackson Middle's soccer team—the Jaguars—were dribbling and passing a ball between them as they took the same path.

"No," I answered, still trying to make sense of what I'd seen.

We ducked out of the way of a man speeding down the sidewalk on a sky-blue Divvy bike. He rushed to the rental station next to us and shoved his bike into an open slot. Looking at the row of bikes, I kept expecting to see a smudge of gray, or black lightning. But everything was as it should be.

"You know there's a bike lane, right?" Eli yelled at the man walking away.

Glancing to my feet, I said, "You think I'm making this up?"

Eli adjusted his backpack straps. "Heck no. Earlier this week Priyanka said she saw two crows talking to each other."

If something weird happened, people always told Eli. He was the king of weird.

"What do you mean, *talking?*"

As we crossed Ashland Avenue, cars honked their horns, and traffic stood bumper to bumper. People coming and leaving the shops on both sides of the avenue were as loud and noisy as the traffic.

"The way we're talking now," Eli said, a goofy look on his face.

I swallowed the lump in my throat. "What were they saying?"

Eli shrugged. "Priyanka said they spoke in a language she'd never heard before."

"What's your theory?" I asked.

"Sometimes ghosts can inhabit the bodies of the living." Eli grinned as if he'd been waiting for his moment of glory. "I guess they would've wanted to inhabit human bodies, but hey, wandering spirits can't be choosy. Priyanka showed me the video on her phone. For a second you see the two crows facing each other and then the screen turns gray. Even the sound went out."

"Gray?" I asked as we passed the corner store. My eyes landed on the empty crate against the barred window. That was Ernest's spot. He was always around after school, tapping his foot and playing the harmonica tangled in his bushy beard. Not seeing him was one more strange thing to add to an already strange day. Ghosts seemed unlikely, but at this point, they were better than an alien invasion. "Have you heard of anything like this before?"

"No," he said, his voice hopeful, "but I'll do some research this weekend."

We stopped in front of his grandmother's three-story greystone building. Jayla, his little sister, knocked on the window on the top floor and waved at us. She and Eli shared the same freckled face, light brown skin, and hazel eyes. I waved back, and she poked out her tongue at Eli, who grinned at her and poked out his tongue too.

"Are you going to tell your parents?" Eli asked.

I shrugged. "Maybe later."

I didn't want to worry Mama. Besides, *maybe* none of it was real. After listening to Papa's stories about his adventures all my life, *maybe* my imagination was as wild as his. I wouldn't tell my parents for now.

That was my first mistake of many more to come. Had I known what lurked in the shadows that day, then *maybe* I would've made a different choice.

TWO

It was just a dream, right?

I COULD TRUST ELI to keep my secret. He'd seen what went down in fourth grade after I told Tisha Thomas that my father fought a kishi, a creature with a human face on the front side of his head and a hyena on the back side. Tisha had called me a liar and told everyone at our table at lunch. By the end of the day, almost the whole fourth-grade class had made fun of me.

Even though I didn't believe Papa's stories anymore, I still didn't mind them. They were fun but just not something I wanted the entire school to know about. I didn't need that sort of attention again. I felt the same about the color bleeding from the world.

When I got home, Mama was buzzing around the

house like a busy bee as she got ready for work. Soon after I walked in, she kissed the top of my head, and her sweet jasmine perfume whisked up my nose. "How was your day, sweetie?" she asked, which was her codespeak for *tell me all about it.*

"It was good?" I said, but it came out like a question, so I added, "I got an A on my report on Mae Jemison. I was the only one in class who chose the first African American woman astronaut to go to space."

"I'm proud of you, Maya," Mama said as she searched for her car keys, which she found between the sofa cushions. "All that hard work you put into your research paid off."

I gave Mama a sheepish smile, but I felt bad for not telling her about my dizzy spell and seeing the world turn gray. In social studies, Mr. Kim said that history was biased because people left out things they wanted to hide. I'd asked him if that was the same as lying, but instead of answering, he opened up the discussion to everyone in class. We all had different opinions about it. I couldn't make up my mind then, but now I thought maybe it wasn't lying outright, but it wasn't telling the truth either.

"Mama," I asked, my stomach twisted in knots, "have you ever heard of the aurora borealis? It's this thing when electrons collide with the atmosphere and make colorful lights in the sky."

"Yes." Mama plucked up her glasses from a shelf in the linen closet. "What about it?"

I cleared my throat and looked everywhere but her face. "I was just wondering if you'd heard of anything like that happening here."

"I'm pretty sure that only happens around the north and south poles," Mama said, distracted as she slipped into her shoes.

"Where's my stethoscope?" she asked, reaching up to touch her neck where it was draped.

It hung next to her badge, which read

CLARISSE ABEOLA, REGISTERED NURSE

JOHN H. STROGER JR. HOSPITAL OF COOK COUNTY

She laughed. "I would misplace my own head if it wasn't attached to my body."

I eased out a frustrated breath. I didn't know what I expected to find out, but at least I knew that Mama hadn't seen anything weird with the sky around here. "If you lost your head, Mama," I said, pushing the thought out of my mind, "I would help you find that too."

When the grandfather clock in the dining room struck five, Mama groaned and cut her eyes at the front door. She was waiting for Papa to get home before heading to work, but her shift started soon, so she couldn't wait much longer.

"He's never this late." I bit my lip. "He's always back before you leave."

Mama worked evenings at Stroger. She hated working at night, but her *rotten boss* (her words, not mine) loved to give her that shift for that very reason.

"I'm sure your father will be home soon," Mama said, slipping her phone in her purse.

When she was worried, she got this little crease between her eyebrows, the same as me. If you asked anyone who knew us, they'd tell you that I looked a lot like Mama. We had the same golden-brown skin, broad noses, and narrow faces. But I had Papa's dark eyes and his dimples.

"I have to get to work," Mama said. "Don't go outside, and keep the doors locked."

"I know the rules, Mama," I grumbled, my shoulders slumping a little.

After she left, I ate dinner while flipping through the latest volume of *Oya: Warrior Goddess*. I had a sinking feeling in my stomach like fluttering moth wings. The one I sometimes got when Papa was away too long. Add that to the strange thing that happened at school, and I had a right to be jumpy.

Really good structural engineers got to travel the

world, and Papa was the best. Architects drew up plans for buildings, and structural engineers made sure their designs were safe. Papa once checked the cables supporting a bridge three thousand feet above a raging river full of piranhas in Belize. If that kind of structure failed, then you'd become fish bait. Papa's job was to make sure it didn't.

Waiting was torture, so after dinner I stomped upstairs to my room and plopped down on the bed with my laptop. I searched for stories of the sky turning gray, black lightning, and people freezing in time. Most of the stuff I found was wacky and straight out of some science fiction magazine.

"I can't be the only one who's seen something like this," I said, slamming the laptop shut.

The curtains ruffled in the breeze at my window. They matched the gold and green headscarf Oya wore in volume 44, when she snuck into the evil Dr. Z's top-secret lair. After she discovered his army of super soldiers, she whipped off her scarf, revealing hair made of flames that shot out to destroy the bad guys.

"What would *she* do?" I wondered aloud.

Oya wasn't like most superheroes. She wasn't from another planet, and she didn't have fancy gadgets. She was a spirit goddess, an orisha. She controlled wind, lightning, and storms, and never lost a fight. Dr. Z and his cronies called her *that meddling Warrior Goddess*. I knew one thing for sure: she would get to the bottom of whatever was going on. I planned to do the same.

Before getting ready for bed, I peeked out the window. Night settled over the city, and the streetlights sparked to life. There was no sign of color bleeding from the world as people parked their cars after getting off work. The cranky Johnston twins, Miss Ida and Miss Lucille, had come out for their evening stroll.

The twins stooped over matching wood canes and wore matching pink bonnets. Both had deep brown skin and eyes the color of new pennies. They fussed at kids so much that their faces were matching scowls, too.

All of a sudden, they looked straight at me like my thoughts had projected into their minds. Light reflected in their coppery, catlike eyes and made my heart leap against my chest. There was something so strange about them that I could never put my finger on. One of them (I think Miss Ida, but it was hard to tell this far away) waved at me, her mouth set in a hard line. Heat rushed to my cheeks as I waved back. I'd been caught red-handed spying on my neighbors.

I drew the curtains shut in a hurry. Disappointed that Papa hadn't come home, I climbed into bed and stared at the Oya poster on the wall. A tornado circled her body, and instead of flames for hair, she had long black braids that flew in the wind of her storm.

The sinking feeling in my stomach only grew worse. I was too lazy to get up and turn off the light, so I buried my head under my pillow. Right before falling asleep, I grumbled that the light should turn itself off, and it did. At the time, I didn't think much about it. Maybe Papa had come home and switched it off. Or maybe Eli was right about our whole neighborhood being a hotspot for ghosts.

That night I dreamt that I was standing in the middle of the street in front of my house. It was a perfect sunny day, except there was a strange man at the end of the block. He wasn't a man, really; he was a thing of ribbons darker than the darkest night. Sunlight bent around his body, leaving him shrouded in shadows. His skin was the color of the moon, and his pale violet eyes glowed. His ribbons wriggled like a bed of snakes. When they settled around him in waves of black and purple silk, his full body came into view. He was tall, at least ten feet, and I stumbled back a few steps. Besides his appearance, something else was off about him, and he made the hairs stand up on the back of my neck.

The color bled from everything around him. The houses, the trees, the grass, the cars, even the pavement. It all washed away like melting snow. Instead of running down the gutters, it gathered at his feet in a pool and his ribbons drank it. It sounded like someone slurping up noodles but one hundred times worse.

I stood opposite him with my hands balled into fists. My whole body shook. Deep down I wanted to run away, but a fire burned inside me. He was draining the life out of my neighborhood, and I couldn't let him.

"Stop doing that!" I shouted.

The man tilted his head to one side and wagged his finger at me.

"Come closer, child." His voice was cold and sent chills down my spine. But even though he scared me, something in the smoothness of his words reminded me of when Papa sang. "Let me get a good look at you."

"No!" I tried to sound brave. "You don't belong here."

When he stepped closer, the space between us stretched so that I was farther away from him. He smiled at this and shook his head with a gleam in his eyes, like he was scheming up something bad. "Some people never learn."

"Who . . . who are you?" I asked, my voice trembling. "*What* are you?"

"He can't hide you forever," the man said as his ribbons began to wriggle again. "I will find you, and then I will put an end to your miserable little life."

I bolted up in bed in the middle of the night in a puddle of sweat. My breath came out hard and fast as I switched on the lamp.

"It was just a dream," I whispered to myself.

But as I sat there shivering in the dark, it felt real.

THREE

MAYBE THINGS AREN'T REALLY SO BAD

THE NEXT MORNING the smell of pancakes and warm blueberry marmalade lured me from my deep sleep. My head felt foggy, and I couldn't shake the feeling that I was forgetting something important. Something about the lights in my room shutting off, and a man made of shadows. I pushed the thought away as I shoved my feet into my slippers, glad it was finally the weekend.

Pancakes and blueberry marmalade could only mean one thing. I tiptoed out of my room and down the stairs to not wake Mama. A soft whistling filled the hallway. Not the sharp kind that made you wish you had earplugs; this was like sweet birdsong. It stopped when I walked into the kitchen.

Papa stood by the table with a bowl of pancake batter tucked beneath his arm. His locs hung halfway down his back. My hair wasn't as long as his yet, but it was getting close. I spotted flour on his cheek and forehead and forced back a snicker. He always made such a mess.

I ran across the kitchen and wrapped my arms around him. The sinking feeling in my stomach from last night melted away. Papa laughed as he juggled the bowl to the table.

"I'm the luckiest father in the world to receive such a welcome." He dropped to one knee, so his face was level with mine. His expression turned serious, but the twinkle in his dark eyes told me that he was about to say something silly. "Did you keep the banshees out of the house while I was away?"

"Papa!" I rolled my eyes. "Banshees aren't real."

Usually, I would play along for a little while, but I wasn't in the mood after yesterday. *You won't believe what happened!* I almost said. *The world turned gray, my math teacher froze like a Popsicle, then everything went back to normal.* In hindsight, that didn't exactly sound newsworthy or as interesting as any of his stories.

Papa raised an eyebrow. "What's wrong, Maya?"

"You're late." I crossed my arms. "I was worried."

"Sometimes my work takes longer than I expect," Papa said.

"Why can't you find a job in Chicago?" I asked. "Then you wouldn't have to go away."

"If we shun our responsibilities, who will make sure that the work gets done?" Papa answered, coming to his feet. "You're still too young to understand, Maya, but I have a very important job that no one else can do."

"Papa, I'm twelve," I said. "I'm not too young to understand."

"You're like a hatchling, so new to the world." He ruffled my hair. "Are you hungry?"

I let out a frustrated sigh because (a) he didn't take my question seriously and (b) he compared me to a *hatchling*. Who called their kid a hatchling? But the pancakes were, in fact, calling my name. My stomach growled as I plopped down at the table.

Papa set a plate of pancakes smothered in blueberry marmalade in front of me. As I started to dig in, he put another batch on the griddle and winked. "For Mama when she gets up." He wiped his forehead with the back of his hand, smearing more flour on his dark skin, and I laughed. I couldn't be mad at him for long. "I have a surprise for you."

When he said *surprise,* my heart rate doubled. He reached in the front pocket of his apron and handed me two pieces of paper. I stared down at them, not believing my eyes.

"Comic-Con tickets?" I almost yelped but lowered my voice to not wake Mama.

"It's about time I take you," Papa said, beaming. "You're old enough now."

I didn't have the heart to tell him that kids younger than me went to cons all the time.

"Thank you, Papa." I bounced on my chair. I begged him for tickets last year, but he said that he would take me when I was older. I thought he meant *much* older, not a *year later* older. "Why did you change your mind?"

"It wasn't an easy decision," he said, his face a little sad. "But you're growing up fast, and you're not going to stay my little girl forever."

Papa ruffled my hair again as I stuffed pancakes into my mouth. I wondered which of my Oya costumes I would wear to Comic-Con. The black one with the gold studs down the sleeves, or the red one with the matching cape? Or I could get a new one. I had almost a month to decide. "How was your trip?" I asked.

"I could have done without mosquitos the size of bats in South America." Papa shuddered. "You have to sleep under a net in the jungle and wear repellent made from the slime of a Peruvian slug to ward them off."

I frowned. "Why were you in the jungle?"

Papa shrugged, sticking out his lips. "I was patching up an old dam."

"In the jungle?" I laced my voice with sarcasm. "Are there dams in the middle of nowhere?"

"A jungle isn't the middle of nowhere," Papa retorted. "Besides, I soon found out that the mosquitos were the least of my worries." He put Mama's pancakes in the microwave for later, then sat down across from me. His face looked tired, and he had dark circles under his eyes. "I was minding my own business, setting up my tent for the night, when I heard a sound on the wind."

"Is this another story about the impundulu?" I said through a mouthful of pancakes. They were magical giant birds that had sharp spikes like fishbones on their bellies. They hardly ever flew, but when they did, their wings sounded like helicopter blades.

He shook his head. "That's another story for another time."

Papa loved telling stories. Impundulu, kishi, were-hyenas, the time he beat LeBron James one-on-one. Or when he paraglided over Mont Blanc in France and ended up at Buckingham Palace in England. No twelve-year-old believed stories like that—not with the internet to debunk them. His stories were no more real than the Loch Ness monster or Bigfoot, but they always made me want to see more of the world.

I swallowed down my pancakes, then asked, "What sort of sound did you hear?"

"Bells like the sweet melodies from my youth." Papa got a dreamy look before he cleared his throat. "But these bells lulled me into a deep trance, and before I knew it, I was walking from camp barefooted. I tumbled through the bush, cringing at the howls of dangerous creatures in the night. All I could think about was those little bells."

I narrowed my eyes. "Where did they come from?"

Papa stared into space, his face blank. He always did that when telling a story, and no matter how many times he did, my heart sped up waiting for his next words. I was such a sucker.

His voice dropped low, and a shiver crawled down my spine. "I got this creepy feeling that I was being watched, but it was too dark to see anything. All I knew was that the bells had bewitched me and, no matter how much I fought, I couldn't break their spell."

"What happened?" I asked, on the edge of my seat.

"I saw the elokos in a clearing," Papa said, his voice dropping even lower.

"What are elokos?" I frowned.

"They're dangerous forest folk with an appetite for human flesh," Papa said.

I squinted at him. "What do these elokos look like?"

"Hmm, they're about this tall." He motioned his hand to the height of a fourth grader. "And they have razor-sharp teeth, pointy ears, and scaly green skin. They communicate with each other through thoughts."

"Like telepaths?" I had learned the word in school.

Papa nodded. "I didn't come out of my trance until they stopped ringing their bells, but by then, they had strung me up between two trees and lit a fire. They were preparing to cook me with my clothes and all. No matter how much I pleaded, they wouldn't let me go. Knowing that I was going to die, I decided to sing. I needed something to keep my mind off the fire about to roast me alive."

I put my fork aside, waiting for him to tell me it was all a joke. But then Papa started to sing at the table. His usual deep voice dropped into a familiar lullaby.

From the morning's glow to the evening's low
There's much work to do and many places to go
But no matter how far I travel or the people I see
There's nowhere in the whole world I'd rather be
For though I must fight to hold the beasts at bay
No mountain or storm or foe will keep me away
For I'll cross raging rivers and bend hyperspace
Just to see a smile on my sweet baby girl's face

I couldn't hold back my smile. If I thought Papa's voice was magical when he told stories, it was mesmerizing when he sang.

"The elokos stopped what they were doing and stood like statues," Papa said. "My song had hypnotized them the same as their bells had done to me. The fire still hadn't reached my backside, so I wiggled my way free. All through my singing, the elokos didn't move a muscle. I knew if I stopped, my spell over them would break and I'd be in big trouble again. So I ran back to camp and kept singing the whole way. Thankfully, my voice lasted until morning and by then the elokos had disappeared."

"Papa." I glanced down at the smear of marmalade left on my empty plate. "I know there aren't really any elokos and you're just making up this story."

"Oh, is that so?" His eyebrows shot up like he was surprised. "How do you know?"

I took a deep breath. He'd been telling such wild stories for so long that even seeing the color bleed from the world seemed ordinary. I *really* should have told him about what happened at school, but as silly as it sounded, it felt good to have a secret of my own. "Maybe some of it *is* true," I said. "Like maybe you really were in the jungle."

Papa shifted in his chair, his face turning serious. "I admit that I may embellish my stories a little, but I tell them for a reason, Maya. The world isn't always what it seems. You understand that, don't you?"

I sat a little straighter and looked him square in the eyes. "Yes, Papa, I understand," I said, even though I really didn't.

FOUR

WHEN SHADOWS TURN
INTO WRITHING SNAKES

I STOOD ACROSS FROM PAPA with my staff ready to strike. Our neighbors' dog, Lucky, poked his nose through the fence separating our backyards. His tail wagged as he looked back and forth between Papa and me. With all the treats I'd given him, Lucky *should* have been on my side. But ever since Papa brought him that peanut butter and jelly bone, he'd defected.

"Traitor," I hissed at him.

The golden retriever stuck out his tongue, leaving no doubt whose side he was on.

Narrowing my eyes, I turned my attention back to the match. Papa circled my position. Maybe other kids liked to spend their Saturday afternoons hanging out with their friends or playing video games, but this was my favorite time with Papa. We'd been practicing staff play since fourth grade, and I'd gotten a lot better at figuring out his next move. He always got a twinkle in his eyes when he was about to try some fancy footwork. When he went for a straightforward strike, he usually had a silly grin like now.

I shifted the staff so that it was alongside my body with my arm tucked in close. It was almost as long as I was tall and made of smooth oak, with knots where the tree limbs had once been. The wood was reddish-brown and polished, and easy to handle. Papa's staff was a head taller than me and as black as night, with white writing painted on it. When I was little, he used to point out the symbols and tell me what they meant.

Unlike with alphabets, each symbol had several meanings. A leopard with raised paws had a different meaning than a leopard leaping or one sitting. To make things more complicated, the exact meaning depended on the symbols around it.

So the symbols for the sun, tree with leaves, and a leopard with raised paws meant *I walk with courage*. Like the leopard, a tree had different meanings too, depending on if it had leaves or not. A tree with leaves represented *movement*. A tree without leaves meant *to stay in one place*. There were hundreds of symbols on the staff, and I couldn't remember what they all meant.

Lucky barked, catching my attention for a split second, and Papa attacked. I almost didn't have time to block. Going on the defense like he taught me, I ducked, sweeping my staff in a long arc, and slipped behind him. But Papa was too quick as he twisted around and struck twice more. I parried right, then left, but caught a tap on my shoulder for moving too slow.

"You're distracted today, Maya," he said as our staffs connected a fourth time.

He was right. I couldn't stop thinking about yesterday. To make matters worse, I kept remembering the man in shadows from my dream. His slippery smile taunted me.

I took the offense with a one-two-three strike combo. Learning how to handle a staff was Papa's idea. After I'd begged him to sign me up for the dojo down the street, he insisted on teaching me how to use a staff. He said that he learned when he was young, and he was so excited about teaching me that I couldn't say no. Even if it wasn't exactly self-defense, I was learning how to be quick on my feet and dodge attacks. So instead of taking *normal classes* like a *normal kid,* I got to spar with my father in my backyard. Not that I was complaining. I liked having a staff of my own, and it was fun.

A shiver shot down my back when I thought about the man from my dreams again. It would be easy for one of his writhing ribbons to trap me like a fly in a spider's web. Thankfully it was just a nightmare, but that didn't make him any less scary. "A staff won't matter in a real fight," I said, concluding that it would be nothing against him.

Papa raised an eyebrow. "How do you know?"

"Because knives and guns and other things are more dangerous," I answered. Emphasis on *other things*. "We can't defend against them—or something even worse—with a staff."

Papa struck again, and the force pushed me back. "That's true. Sometimes it wouldn't be enough." Then he held his staff in front of him. He never went anywhere without it, even when he left for work. "This is my lucky staff," he said. "It's always served me well."

I didn't mean to insinuate that his staff was useless. It was actually pretty cool, especially the way the sun made the symbols shimmer. "Your staff is good," I said, going on the attack, "but mine is better."

Papa looked surprised, then his face transformed into pride. He struck back without warning, but I was ready for him and thrust my staff out to catch his blow. Then I stepped to the side and the momentum of his strike pulled him forward, while I was already clear of his path. He'd taught me how to face an opponent much bigger and stronger than myself. Now I couldn't stop grinning. Soon I'd be as good as him or better.

"Good work, Maya." Papa laughed. "You're a quick learner, but don't get too cocky."

Before I could say anything, a piercing boom shook the ground so hard that I almost lost my balance. Car alarms went off on the streets, and Lucky barked. A flock of birds flew in a panic from the tree in our backyard. Papa's face turned a little gray, and his mouth settled into a hard line. He looked *afraid*.

Papa was never scared, or more than mildly upset. At that moment, I realized that he wasn't invincible, no matter if in all his stories he always outwitted his foes. A tremble crept up my arms as I leaned on my staff for balance. The fact that Papa was afraid made me scared too.

"Was that an earthquake?" I asked, my voice quiet.

I'd never heard of an earthquake causing such a loud boom. They weren't common in the Midwest, and definitely not Chicago. At least there didn't seem to be any real damage. One by one the cars stopped blaring as people turned off their alarms.

"It sure felt like one." Papa tightened his grasp on his staff and looked around as if he expected someone to appear out of thin air. "I have to leave again tonight," he said, rushing his words.

"You just got back!" My voice was so high-pitched that I sounded like a little kid. "Can't you stay the whole weekend?"

"My work is never-ending," he said, his face stern. "There's much I must do."

"Can't someone else do it for a little while, Papa?" I begged. "Why is it always you?"

Papa winced. "I told you already, Maya, I'm the only one who can."

He always gave the same answer, so I asked, "What's so important about your work?"

Papa frowned and said, "I promise I'll tell you very soon."

Mama had a shift at the hospital again. She went through her usual routine of looking for her misplaced car keys and purse, and Papa helped her. When she was almost out the door, he wrapped his arms around her, and she leaned against his chest. They stayed like that for a long time. Neither said a word.

"Be safe," Mama whispered. "Okay?"

"Always," Papa answered.

My cheeks warmed watching them, so I stared at the TV instead.

Soon after Mama left, Papa announced that it was time for him to go too. I would be home alone again. I wasn't scared, but I wished the three of us could spend more time together.

"Will you be back in time for Comic-Con?" I asked, biting my lip.

"Of course, I will." Papa knelt in front of the couch where I sat. "I wouldn't miss taking you to see Oya, the great warrior goddess. If we're lucky, we'll get a picture of the two of you."

My heart lit up at that idea, but I wouldn't let it distract me from my plans.

Papa got dressed in his usual multicolored shirt (this one red with penguins on it), jeans, and a dark coat. After he left to walk to the train, I counted to ten, then followed him. Mama would usually drive him to the airport, but with the car gone, he'd have to take the orange line to Midway. I knew I was breaking Mama's number one rule (*don't ever leave the house alone at night*), but something wasn't right. Papa never left again so soon, and he was upset after the earthquake this morning. Not only that, he'd paced back and forth and stared out the window all day. He even took a private call upstairs in the middle of lunch. I didn't have much of a plan, but maybe I'd get lucky and overhear something on the way to the train.

As I hurried down the sidewalk, shadows crawled in the places where the streetlights didn't reach. There were a few people out, but the streets were mostly empty. If Papa or Mama knew that I'd left home alone after dark, they would ground me for a month. Even worse, they might take away my Comic-Con tickets, so I had to be extra careful.

Papa kept looking around, almost like he expected something to happen. It was eerily quiet, and I got that queasy feeling in my stomach again. A little voice in my head told me to go home, but I didn't listen.

The longer I followed Papa, the more things didn't feel right. The darkness seemed to almost breathe on its own. I forced myself to keep going as the shadows grew closer. "It's just your imagination," I whispered.

But I didn't believe it was my imagination when Papa stepped into a curtain of shadows and vanished. I stopped cold, and my hand flew to my mouth to cut off a scream. The shadows had swallowed him up.

They *swallowed* him.

"Papa?" I snapped out of my shock and rushed after him, but he was gone.

My breath came out hard and fast, and my lips trembled.

I turned around and looked everywhere. There was no sign of him. My heart thundered against my chest, and goose bumps lit on my arms. The shadows pressed in around me and felt slick against my face. I could smell them too. They stank like rotten eggs.

When I backed away, something reached out of the dark and grabbed my wrist. Cold seared into my skin. I tried to free myself, but the thing only tugged harder. Shadows like writhing snakes crawled up my arm—and I knew it was *him*. The man from my nightmare. Come to make good on his threat to kill me.

I clawed at the shadows with my other hand, only they slithered up that arm too. I screamed, and the darkness muted my voice. When I kicked, my foot connected with air.

Pain shot up my arms. My hands had gone numb. Frost started to creep across my skin. I wriggled my stiff fingers, and the ice crystals cracked and shattered. Then, with all my strength, I closed my hands around the shadows, which felt like thick ropes. I was sure they would turn me into an ice cube, but I gritted my teeth and jerked my arms back even harder. This time it worked.

I was barely free before someone grabbed my shoulder. I tried to pull away, but the person held on tight and stopped me in my tracks. A hot breeze whipped against my neck as a piercing screech rang out in the night. I flinched when the shadows recoiled and disappeared into the darkness.

Before I had time to sigh in relief, the person spun me around. I stared up at my cranky neighbor, Miss Ida Johnston. I knew it was her, not Miss Lucille, because of the mole over her left eye. She glared down at me with a look that said I was in big trouble.

Five

When I face something
worse than shadows

Miss Ida narrowed her eyes into slits that made her look like an iguana. Her hand was still clamped down on my shoulder in an iron grip, and my whole body trembled beneath her touch. I couldn't stop thinking about Papa and how he'd disappeared into the shadows.

"Did you see that?" I asked, my voice shaking.

She let go of me and massaged her forehead like I was giving her a headache. That was when I noticed that she didn't have her cane. "What are you going on about?"

"The shadows," I said, realizing how silly it sounded out loud. "They tried . . ."

I still could feel an ache from where they'd climbed up

my arms. Their touch was colder than the worst Chicago winter, so cold that it burned. I couldn't stop wiggling my fingers to make sure they still worked. "You had to see them."

Miss Ida frowned. "Stop letting your imagination get away with you, Maya."

"It wasn't my imagination," I yelled.

Oh no, I shouldn't have done that.

I cringed as Miss Ida raised one eyebrow and cocked her head to the side.

"See what happens when you aren't where you're supposed to be?" she said, her voice full of venom. "Your parents would skin your hide if they knew you were out this late."

"Didn't you hear me scream?" I asked, my voice hoarse.

"Of course," Miss Ida said. "That's why I came to see what the commotion was. I saw you standing there like you'd lost your good sense. What in the heavens are you doing out here?"

I shouldn't have expected Miss Ida to believe me. Who had ever heard of shadows coming to life? That kind of thing only happened in scary movies. "I was looking for someone," I said, not telling the whole truth.

Even if Miss Ida didn't believe me, what I saw was real. I set my jaw, glaring into the dark. I was going to figure out why all these weird things were happening in my neighborhood, and next time, I'd be ready.

Miss Ida shook her head and rolled her eyes. "Come on, you're going straight home."

As she ushered me down the street, sweat drenched my clothes and the night air chilled me to the bone. I glanced over my shoulder and could've sworn that the shadows moved again.

For someone who hadn't seen anything, Miss Ida looked over her shoulder a lot too.

At school, I did a lot of staring out the window, so much that two teachers threatened to put me in detention if I didn't stop. After Miss Ida had marched me home Saturday night, I called Papa. His voicemail kept picking up. I tried again and again until finally he answered. He immediately thought something was wrong, and I made up an excuse for calling so he wouldn't worry. He said that he was boarding a plane. I could hear all the noise in the background and the wind whipping against the phone. He was okay. That was all that mattered. The shadows hadn't gotten him, but they *were* real.

In science class, Eli, Frankie, and I worked on a group project together, as in Frankie did the work while we watched. Science was her specialty. Her prescription goggles covered up most of her face and made her eyes look huge. She wore her hair in two puffy pigtails, one on either side of her head. Whereas Eli had pale skin and light eyes, Frankie had deep brown skin and eyes almost as dark as my own.

"You could've been sleepwalking," she said in her squeaky voice after I told them what happened Saturday. "It's more common than people think. My mom says it happens to fifteen percent of the population."

Between Frankie and both her moms, they had enough IQ to invent interstellar space travel. But science couldn't explain the writhing shadows, nor the world turning gray. "I wasn't sleeping while standing in front of the chalkboard."

Frankie frowned as she bent over her experiment. That was her thinking face, and I knew her computer brain was hard at work on another theory. While she fiddled with the copper wires and batteries, Eli played on his phone.

"I took some pictures this weekend," he said. "I didn't see anything paranormal in them, but I'm convinced that we're dealing with a ghost invasion."

Frankie quirked an eyebrow at that. "Where's your concrete evidence of *ghosts?*"

"Where's your concrete evidence that dark matter really exists?" Eli shot back.

"Well, actually . . ." Frankie's face lit up. "Scientists can measure it, so we know it's real."

Eli slapped his forehead. "Why did I even ask?"

"I don't know the right answer," I said, "but I plan to get to the bottom of this."

"I'll help," they both chimed.

I was in enough trouble already, but there was no way around it. I had to figure out what was happening in my neighborhood. "I'm going back outside tonight after my mom leaves for work."

Eli sank in his chair. "It's bingo night at the community center, and Nana is hosting, which means I'm stuck officiating. There's no way she'll let me out of it. Plus, Jayla and I spent a day making brownies for the players. She'll have a fit if I don't come."

"I'll come with you," Frankie said, barely holding back a smile. "I want to test a theory."

"Miss Abeola." Mr. Jenkins's eyes landed on me as he approached our table. His black-rimmed glasses had slipped to the end of his nose, and he had his hair braided in cornrows. He frowned as he noticed my lack of progress. Frankie had finished, and Eli had at least uncoiled his copper wire and stacked his batteries. The copper wire in front of me was still coiled up, and the pack of batteries unopened. "I would hate to have to email your parents and tell them you're slacking off in my class."

Mama was already going to ground me as soon as Miss Ida told her about Saturday night. I didn't need more trouble. "I was thinking of my hypothesis before getting started, sir," I droned.

Mr. Jenkins glanced up at the clock. "It's fifteen minutes until the end of class, and you spent all this time thinking about your hypothesis?"

"Actually, sir," Frankie butted in, "Maya and Eli helped me conceptualize the design on *our* three-tier dimmer, so that's why they're both behind."

Mr. Jenkins's eyes lit up when he saw Frankie's work. "Class, gather around and see what Miss Williams has created," he said. "As always she's demonstrated a mastery of science."

Not only had Frankie powered two light bulbs, she'd built a switch using a penny and wires to turn them on and off. The other kids stood around our table asking Frankie how she did it. She grinned, happy to explain her process in painstaking detail.

After the bell rang, Mr. Jenkins raised his voice over the noise of kids packing up. "Tomorrow we'll practice making lightning in a jar—one of my favorite activities."

Lucky for me, Mr. Jenkins seemed to have forgotten about his threat to email my parents.

Frankie waited in the hallway while I told Ms. Vander-bilt that I didn't feel well, and she let me out of tutoring. I expected a speech about keeping up with my studies, but she had three times as many papers on her desk to grade than last week. Once I was in the clear, Frankie and I headed for my house.

When I walked in the door, I braced myself in case Miss Ida had told Mama about the other night. Instead Mama asked if Frankie and I could help her find her missing shoes. We checked in all the closets and the pantry and found them underneath a pile of laundry.

"Mama, can Frankie stay for dinner?" I said, hopeful.

She glanced between the two of us like she knew we were up to something. Then her cellphone vibrated against the living room table, which distracted her. "As long as you girls behave, okay?"

Frankie and I both said, "Yes, ma'am."

Once Mama left, we ran upstairs to my room to come up with a plan.

"Now we go shadow hunting," I said. I was a little excited and a lot scared, but I wasn't going to hide from whatever attacked me on the street. Maybe I didn't know what had Papa upset, but I could figure this out.

"We need a flashlight," Frankie said, "and a whistle."

"I get the flashlight for the dark, but why the whistle?"

"Actually, the flashlight will test my theory," Frankie said. "Shadows can't exist where there's light, so the flashlight should act as a repellent. It'll be like bug spray for mosquitos."

"What if it's something else?" I asked. "What if it's not shadows?"

"You said a loud screech scared them away before," Frankie said.

"The whistle is to scare *them* away," I said, my eyebrows shooting up. "You're a genius."

Frankie scratched her forehead. "Well, technically I am—"

"Never mind." I raced down the hall to get flashlights from the storage closet.

Frankie was in the middle of explaining light theory when we heard the cranky twins through the window. Neither of them had their canes as they unloaded groceries from their SUV. In fact, both twins looked like they'd never had any trouble walking in their entire lives. Seeing this, Frankie frowned at me, and I shrugged. I couldn't explain it either.

I narrowed my eyes, remembering two nights ago. No way Miss Ida hadn't seen the shadows. She was right there. "There's something weird going on with the Johnston twins."

"I know that face." Frankie adjusted her glasses. "What are you scheming?"

"I think they know something," I said. "Let's see what they're up to tonight."

With that, we tweaked our original plan. After a quick

dinner, we waited until nightfall and set out to follow the cranky twins. I brought my staff just in case. You can never be too careful with hungry shadows on the loose. We stayed a full block behind the sisters and didn't use our flashlights, so we wouldn't draw their attention. They walked fast, and I didn't expect two elderly women to move as well as they did without their canes. They peeped down alleyways and in abandoned lots, searching for something. It was clear they weren't out for a casual night stroll.

"What do you think he's going to do?" Miss Ida asked, her words carried on the wind.

That was definitely Miss Ida, because her voice was huskier than Miss Lucille's.

"He'll do what he always does," Miss Lucille answered. "Handle the darkbringers."

Frankie and I both looked at each other, our eyes wide.

"Darkbringers," I mouthed. "Have you heard of them?"

Frankie shook her head. "Sounds like a new gang."

"What if he can't stop the veil from failing this time?" Miss Ida asked, voice desperate.

I wondered who *he* was. Some of the proverbs on my father's staff mentioned a veil. But I'd never thought to ask what it meant, and now I was seriously regretting it.

"The veil is very old," Miss Lucille said. "It's bound to fail one day."

There was a long pause, then Miss Ida said, "I'm not looking forward to another war."

Frankie grabbed my arm and stopped me in my tracks. My mouth dropped open as the words *another war* ran circles in my mind. I imagined the twins in an actual war. Maybe they were fighter pilots, or sergeants yelling at cadets about untied shoelaces.

"This doesn't feel right," Frankie said, hugging her shoulders. "I think we should go back."

Even in the dim moonlight, I saw that Frankie was shaking. Last year, when Eli swore the stairs at school were haunted, she debunked his claim by proving that a faulty air duct, not a ghost, was causing a cold spot. Frankie had an explanation for everything. If she was scared, then we were in trouble.

The streetlight flickered, and we both flinched. In the short time that we'd stopped, the twins had vanished around a corner. An eerie silence settled over the neighborhood. Even the sound of rats in the garbage cans and the hum of water in the drains along the street faded away.

"I think you're right." My palm was slick with sweat against my staff. "We should probably go back."

Before we could make a step, there was a *zing* like static in the air and the streetlight went out. Frankie switched on her flashlight first, and I fumbled to turn on mine as one by one all the lights on the block shut off.

"Maybe a transistor blew," Frankie said, sweeping her flashlight in a wide arc. "That would cause all the lights to go out at once."

"What was that?" I pointed my flashlight in time to see a pack of dogs trot into an alley. At least, what looked like dogs. I'd never seen dogs with ears that round and brown spots all over their coats. Their movements were very undoglike, and it made the hairs prick on the back of my neck. "I really think we should go now."

Frankie yelped, and I almost jumped out of my skin. She stared down at her elbow, and I beamed my flashlight on her. "Something cold touched my arm."

Shadows or not, something was stalking our neighborhood. "Did the light work . . ."

I stopped midsentence as a shadow whipped out from the darkness. I jerked back, but not fast enough. The shadow slashed against my cheek. "Ahhh," I screamed, and stumbled out of reach. Frankie wasn't so lucky. The shadow snapped around her wrist. She shrieked as her flashlight crashed against the ground and the light blinked out.

"No!" I fumbled for the whistle around my neck. My fingers were clumsy, and I kept dropping it. When I finally got it to my lips, I blew, but it didn't work. More shadows grabbed Frankie from behind, dragging her away from me. I couldn't let them take her.

Gritting my teeth, I swung my flashlight as hard as I could. I got Frankie into this mess, and I had to do something. I wanted to use my staff, but I'd tucked it under my arm so I could switch on the flashlight. The light bounced everywhere, even blinding me for a second, as I swung again. This time I made contact with something and the impact vibrated up my arm. The shadows hissed, low and menacing. I kept swinging until they let go and Frankie crashed into my shoulder. She stared at me wide-eyed. She had icicles on her hands and her T-shirt. We were both shaking. Turned out it wasn't a good idea to sneak out at night looking for trouble after all.

We ran. Maybe we should've paid attention to which direction, but we didn't care as long as it was away from the shadows. With the flashlight bouncing around, we couldn't see our way and ended up in an alley. When we stopped to catch our breaths, I leaned over with my hands on my knees.

Frankie wiped sweat from her forehead. "I think we can now say with confidence that those are *not* in fact shadows," she said. "But there has to be another logical explanation."

I stared at her with my mouth open. Of course *she* would try to come up with a new theory in the middle of fleeing from an unknown foe. I searched for a snappy comeback to ease the tension, but my breath caught in my throat. The *dogs* I saw earlier trotted into the alleyway with their sharp teeth bared. I swallowed hard as Frankie and I backed away. "I don't think those are dogs."

"Those are definitely not dogs," she said, her voice squeaky. "Hyenas?"

I nodded, almost unable to speak. "Maybe they escaped from Brookfield Zoo?"

As the hyenas closed in on us, I glanced over my shoulder at the wall at our backs. Our only way out was to climb it or go through the pack of hyenas, who were licking their lips. The wall was too high, and there was no time to prop something against it to give us a boost.

"Take this," I said, thrusting the flashlight into Frankie's hand.

I banged the tip of my staff against the pavement, hoping I could scare the hyenas away, but they kept coming.

"Try the whistle," Frankie said, leaning so close to me that our shoulders bumped.

"I would if I hadn't lost it when we ran," I said, my heart racing against my chest.

"Oh," she gasped.

It wasn't until they stepped out of the shadows that I realized the hyenas had grown bigger. They stood on their hind legs, and their claws looked like curled knives. Their torsos stretched into a shape that was unmistakable and impossible. These were *werehyenas,* like from Papa's stories, half hyena, half man. But it couldn't be. Those were just make-believe.

"No way," I mumbled under my breath.

Stories or not, they were here now. Moonlight glinted off their sharp teeth as they sauntered forward, savoring the moment. I stood with my staff, ready to fight them, or as ready as one can be facing down six hungry werehyenas. Then the beasts charged, and Frankie stumbled beside me.

I stepped in front of my friend with the staff crisscrossed over my body and dropped into a crouch, my knees bent. When the werehyenas were almost on top of us, though, something happened. A bright light flashed in the alley. It was so intense that I backed away, shielding my face in the crook of my elbow. I could still hear the hyenas cackling, but they had backed off too. Before I could figure out what the heck was going on, I tripped over something and hit the ground hard.

Six

A perfectly reasonable explanation

I WASN'T DEAD AT LEAST. That was good.

The mysterious bright light had disappeared, and I forced myself to sit up. I had scrapes on my palms, and my butt was sore from the fall. My head was spinning, too. The werehyenas were pacing back and forth a few feet away. I thought for sure they would've eaten us by now. This gave new meaning to playing with your food.

Not taking my eyes off them, I searched for the staff. My hands bumped into slimy things and puddles of what was most certainly *not* water and trash. My vision was still a little fuzzy around the edges after the light. Probably better to not see what I was touching, anyway. My heart raced as the seconds ticked down. I didn't know why the werehyenas hadn't attacked, but I didn't expect that to last either.

"Here," Frankie said, thrusting my staff into my hand.

"What happened?" I asked, half out of breath as she helped me to my feet.

I saw the outline of a faint light that had formed a circle around us. It looked like an electric net made of thousands of tiny lights woven together. It was equal parts fascinating and terrifying. I had no clue what it was, but for now it wasn't trying to hurt us.

"I don't know," Frankie stuttered, looking at her hands in shock. "It's some kind of force field between us and the hyenas, if that's even what you can call them."

Her eyebrows drew together. Nothing stumped Frankie. But after the shadows, the werehyenas, the light, even she couldn't explain this away.

"They're *were*hyenas," I said, "and ten times more dangerous than regular hyenas."

Calling them werehyenas out loud sounded much weirder than in my head. My face felt hot with embarrassment. Papa said that werehyenas came to North America by pretending to be regular hyenas. They let people working for zoos capture them, so they could look for new hunting grounds. A bunch had escaped. Now people mistook them for Bigfoot all the time, who, according to Papa, got a bad rap on account of his size. Was he real too?

"Maybe there was some mind-altering drug in the vanilla pudding at school today," Frankie offered. "My moms say that the government performs secret experiments on people all the time."

"I never eat the pudding." I shook my head. "So that can't be it."

I wondered how this light came to be, but also how it had suddenly grown less intense, less bright, like an afterglow. The werehyenas stopped pacing back and forth. Teeth bared, drool wetting their greedy black lips, they cackled at the moon.

"So much for my mind-altering drug theory." Frankie pushed up her sliding glasses with one shaky hand. "Then my vote is they escaped a government lab where they'd been genetically spliced."

When I cocked my head at her, she added, "You know, when you mix the genes of one species with another one."

"Yes, of course." I rolled my eyes. "I *splice* genes in my spare time."

One of the werehyenas, the biggest of the pack, sauntered closer and sniffed the air. He stopped short of crossing the bubble of light—which seemed to be protecting us from them. The werehyena turned his yellow eyes straight at me as he growled, "We're going to eat you."

"Did that *thing* just talk?" Frankie shrieked. "That's incredible."

Never mind that the *thing* threatened to eat us.

"Do you two ever shut up?" the werehyena snarled.

I tightened my grasp on the staff—getting angrier by the second. My fingers burned from gripping the staff hard, and heat flushed down my arm. I didn't know where the light was coming from or how long it would last, but if it failed, I was ready to fight.

"I know what you are," I said through gritted teeth. I knew even if my mind had a hard time *believing*. I forced myself to slow my breathing like Papa taught me during staff play. I needed total concentration to take on the werehyenas. "We're not afraid of you either."

Under her breath, Frankie whispered, "Speak for yourself. I happen to be very afraid."

"Shush," I hissed back. "He doesn't need to know that."

The werehyena clucked his tongue, his keen ears perked to our every word. He had to be the leader of the pack, since none of the others spoke. He raised himself to stand up straight on his hind legs and stood over six feet tall. Both Frankie and I gulped.

In one quick swipe, he scraped his claws against the force field that separated us from certain death. The noise was sharp, and sparks shot out. Thankfully, the barrier held, but Frankie stumbled back a few steps. She folded over like he had punched her in the belly.

"Are you okay?" I asked, breaking my stance to check on my friend.

"I . . . I don't know," she said, breathing hard and fast. "It feels like something cut me."

The werehyena smiled, and the anger flared inside me. He'd done that to her, but I didn't know how. The light itself was some kind of magic. *Magic.* The thing that adults said was make-believe. Well, all the adults except Papa.

The werehyena turned his glare on me. "Which of you little godlings should I eat first?"

I frowned. Never mind that he'd threatened to eat me again, but what was a godling? My legs trembled, and my pulse drummed so hard against my ears I thought they would explode. My fear didn't stop me from straightening up and shifting my staff back into defense mode. I wasn't going to let him trick me into doing something silly like stepping outside of the light.

"If you want to eat me, then come get me," I said, giving him my meanest glare.

It probably wasn't the best idea to taunt a hungry werehyena, especially a pack of six hungry werehyenas. The leader threw back his head, turned his snout to the moon, and cackled. The others did the same, and then they dropped to all four legs and trotted to the mouth of the alley. Scratch that: it wasn't a good idea to taunt hungry werehyenas who knew that your only way to escape was through them.

"Do you think they're gone?" Frankie asked, finally able to stand straight again.

"Not a chance," I answered, peering after the werehyenas. "They're coming up with a plan, and we need one of our own." I glanced down at my staff. "I'll knock out as many as I can while you run to get help."

"Maya, I don't think that's a good idea." She pointed her flashlight into the night. "Those werehyenas want to eat us, we should run together."

Frankie and I didn't have enough time to argue about the best way to fend off an attack. The werehyenas appeared out of the dark again, charging toward us. The biggest one, the leader, ran the fastest, his yellow eyes glowing.

I decided in that split second how I was going to react. I would duck and roll out of their path, letting their momentum carry them past us. Then I would take out as many legs as I could so they couldn't pursue once we ran.

The werehyenas startled Frankie, and she dropped the flashlight. It hit the ground, and the light died.

Frankie gave me an apologetic grimace, but she had

nothing to be sorry for. This was an impossible situation under impossible circumstances. My hands shook. In fact, my whole body was shaking. Contrary to my brave words, I was scared out of my mind too.

Just as the werehyenas slammed into the barrier, I yelled, "Dive right."

The force field shattered into a million sparks of light, then a lot of things happened at once. I dove left, ready to slam my staff into the first werehyena to cross my path. Their leader angled his charge for me, his sharp teeth bared. My anemia hit, and my head started to swim. My legs swayed. I fought to stay standing. I couldn't lean on my staff for balance because I needed it to fight.

Frankie didn't dive right. Instead, she did something that if I hadn't seen with my own eyes, I wouldn't believe in a thousand years. Light shot out of her hands and slammed into the werehyenas. When it hit them, they hurtled through the air and collided with the ground.

I gasped, half in shock and half in awe.

How did she do that?

Frankie stood completely still and speechless, clearly in shock too.

The werehyenas whimpered as they scrambled to untangle themselves. Once they climbed to their feet again, they backed away, then turned to flee. Their leader glanced over his shoulder at us, glowering, his black lips drawn back to show sharp fangs. He reminded me of every sulking bully who had ever gotten caught in the act. Even as the were-hyenas tucked their tails and fled back into the shadows, his look said that next time we wouldn't be so lucky.

Seven

I learn a secret

FRANKIE AND I stared at each other for a full minute. She finally broke the standoff and looked down at her trembling hands. This was the first time that I'd ever seen her confused and unsure. But to Frankie's credit, she was much calmer than I would've been in her situation. If it was me, I would've been busy shooting lights into the sky like firecrackers just to see how far they'd go.

"How did you do that?" I asked.

Frankie blew out a shaky breath. "Would you believe me if I said I don't know?"

"From the look on your face, yes," I answered. "Did you feel anything when it happened?"

She turned her hands around to examine her palms. "I

felt this pulsing beneath my skin, almost like a heartbeat." She stared at me with wide eyes. "I didn't know to do it . . . It was just instinct. You know when you get a hunch about something? It was like that. I think I created the force field too . . ."

I bounced on my toes, too excited to stand still. "You're officially a mutant."

"Be serious, Maya!" Frankie said, her voice high-pitched. "Everything can be explained by science. The laws of physics, gravity, matter, atoms . . . *This* is impossible."

"Have you heard of a thing called *magic?*" I asked. "It explains the unexplainable."

As soon as I said the words, I knew I had pushed her too far. Frankie didn't deal well with things that couldn't be explained. Her eyes welled with tears. She was taking this harder than I expected. It wasn't every day a science geek found out that she had the power to shoot light out of her hands.

"I know it seems impossible," I said, patting her shoulder, "but I'm glad we're okay."

She nudged her glasses up. "Me too."

"Eli's going to be so mad he missed this," I said as we started home.

"He'll claim it's a conspiracy," Frankie added.

We froze as Miss Ida and Miss Lucille stepped soundlessly out of the shadows. Both wore matching scowls and had their hands on their hips. At the same time, the streetlights flickered back on, and I breathed a sigh of relief.

"Are you hurt?" they asked together, one voice overlapping the other.

"No," we answered back.

And we weren't, aside from a few scratches. Miss Lucille looked me over, and Miss Ida did the same for Frankie. They definitely knew something. I could tell by how nervous they were acting.

"What in the heavens are you doing out here again?" Miss Ida asked me, then turned her glare on Frankie. "You especially should know better than to get caught up in Maya's antics."

My antics! I almost said. *What about you sneaking around out here?*

But I held my tongue so I didn't make things worse. The twins would tell our parents, and we'd both be grounded for the summer. An awful feeling sank in my chest at the thought. I'd been lucky that Miss Ida hadn't told Mama the first time she caught me out at night.

"We were performing empirical research," Frankie said, speaking up first.

"What?" Miss Lucille said, her face puzzled.

I was pretty sure she didn't expect an answer, but

Frankie took her seriously. "Empirical research is when you try to learn something by experiencing it or observing it. In this case, we were—"

"Enough!" Miss Ida shouted. "You're both in big trouble."

"Did you see the werehyenas too?" I asked.

Both twins went rigid. Miss Lucille's expression was unreadable for someone who grimaced so much. Miss Ida was less careful. I could see the fear in her eyes. Whatever was going on in our neighborhood, they definitely knew about it. Was that why they always took late night walks? Had the twins been looking for the werehyenas earlier? Instead of answering my question, Miss Lucille pointed toward home.

"March," Miss Ida said, and we did.

There was no talking on the way back. Frankie and I exchanged a glance, and I bet that she was thinking the same thing. All clues pointed to two old ladies in matching pink bonnets who had always been a little suspicious. One of these days I would ask them how they could now walk without their canes, but that was best for another time.

Miss Lucille kept her eyes on us while Miss Ida peered into the dark corners and alleys. They both were jumpy. Twice they whispered something to each other in a language I didn't recognize. The words were flowery and slid together like a song.

It was nice and calmed my nerves until I saw Papa

standing in front of our house. He'd only been gone since Saturday night and never came back so soon after leaving. His face was grim, and Miss Lucille and Miss Ida looked like they were the ones in trouble.

"Take Frankie home, please," Papa said. His voice was ice, and I'd never heard him use that tone with anyone. He was going to ground me for the entirety of seventh grade, or until high school, or maybe for life.

"Good luck," Frankie whispered before she left with the Johnston twins.

"Papa, I . . ."

His sharp look cut me off. "Upstairs, Maya."

Without another word, I marched up the stairs and into our house. At least Mama hadn't come home yet. I couldn't bear to face both of them. I started to flop down on the sofa, but Mama would kill me if I got alley muck all over it. Papa let me clean up, then I crept back into the living room where he sat in his recliner.

"I'm sorry, Papa," I said, unable to hold his hard stare. "I know I shouldn't have gone out at night. I shouldn't have broken the rules, but—"

"There's no but, Maya," Papa said.

"I know, but—"

"I said no *but*s," Papa snapped. "You could've been hurt."

"We were attacked by werehyenas, like from your stories," I said, feeling foolish.

"Tell me everything." Papa sucked in a deep breath. "From the beginning."

Which beginning? The beginning when I stood at the chalkboard while black lightning cut across the sky? The beginning in which a man made of ribbons drained the color from our neighborhood in a dream? The beginning when shadows reached out of the darkness and grabbed my arms? The beginning when werehyenas threatened to eat me and my friend?

Papa grimaced as he listened to my story, but he didn't say I was making it up. I told him everything. Everything that was real. The man made of shadows was only a bad dream, and I didn't want to talk about him. He still scared me.

"Maya, I'm disappointed that you didn't tell any of this to me and your mother before now." Papa leaned forward, his elbows digging into his knees. "I know that I haven't been completely open with you about my job, but it was to keep you safe. What you did tonight was dangerous."

I glanced at my feet. He was right. I messed up and had almost gotten Frankie and myself eaten by mythical beasts in the process.

"I know, Papa," I said.

"I don't have much time." He frowned. "I left in the middle of urgent work that I must get back to . . . but I need to tell you something about my job."

My belly flopped. He was leaving again.

Whatever Papa was about to say, it had something to do with all the weird stuff happening. He didn't seem surprised by anything I said—not the world turning gray or the werehyenas.

"Remember I told you I'm a structural engineer, yes?" he said.

I nodded but dared not interrupt in case he decided not to tell me.

"My specialty isn't buildings." Papa sighed. "I'm the guardian of the veil."

When I frowned, he added, "Think of it as an invisible barrier that keeps our world safe from creatures much worse than werehyenas."

My heart raced at this news, and two things jumped out at me. First, *the veil*. The symbols on his staff: the sun, a leopard with raised paws, and a river. I remembered what it meant now: *I am the guardian of the veil*. Miss Lucille and Miss Ida said that the veil was failing and that *he* would handle the darkbringers. I wouldn't have guessed the twins were talking about Papa.

"Guardian of *our world*," I said, almost afraid to know. "What other world is there?"

"The Dark," he said, his voice dropping low. His words hung in the air between us, and the tick-tock of the grandfather clock was the only sound in the house. It counted down to some horrible truth that was stranger than any of his stories.

"Is that where the darkbringers live?" I asked, and Papa flinched.

"Yes," he said, his eyes worried. "The veil is ancient, Maya. Usually when there is a tear, it repairs itself much like a scab grows over a small cut. But time has weakened it, and some tears are too deep to heal on their own. I mend those parts of the veil that can't fix themselves. It's hard to explain how, but think about the way you would patch up a hole in a blanket by sewing a piece of cloth over it. That's what I do and what it means to be the guardian."

This was way too much information to take in at once. Excitement and fear coursed through my chest. It was like someone had plucked my wildest dream (or nightmare) from my head and breathed life into it. But I was also scared because I remembered what the twins said about the war. Holes in *this* veil were why all the weird things had been happening in our neighborhood. Something had slipped through into *our* world.

"I'll tell you more when I get back." Papa stood up. "There's trouble brewing, and I must stop it before it's too late. No time is safe, but I need you to promise me, Maya, that you won't go outside at night alone or with your friends again, okay? The enemy is strongest under the cover of darkness."

I jumped to my feet too. I didn't protest about him leaving or about not going outside. After the werehyenas, I didn't want to meet these darkbringers. "I promise."

"It's complicated," Papa sighed, "but by the time we go to Comic-Con, you'll understand everything."

I didn't understand what Comic-Con had to do with the veil and his job, and there were more important questions on my mind.

"Does Mama know that you're guardian of this veil?" I asked, and he nodded.

"I think I saw a darkbringer in my dreams," I finally confessed. "He was made of shadows."

Papa grimaced and put his hands on my shoulders. They weren't steady and strong like usual; instead, they shook. Only a little, but it was enough to make my knees wobbly as if I'd caught his fear like a common cold. "Maya, this is important," he said. "What else do you recall about the dream? Was he close to you or far away?"

I told him everything I could remember.

"He's no darkbringer." Papa glanced to the floor, looking defeated. "He's the Lord of Shadows, their master."

"He sounds like something out of my comic books," I said, thinking Papa was joking, but he wasn't. Whoever or *whatever* this man was, he scared my father too.

"He's as real as you or I," Papa explained. "He's trapped

in the Dark, but he can enter our world through dreams —which are crossroads between our two worlds."

"I don't understand," I said. "How do you know this Lord of Shadows?"

Pain settled on Papa's face. The Lord of Shadows and my father had history, and it wasn't anything good. "He's taken too much from me to bear, Maya," Papa mumbled, almost to himself. "One day I will tell you that story too."

After an uncomfortable silence, Papa grabbed his staff from beside the recliner. "I have to go now," he said, "but I want you to keep my staff." He flashed me a reassuring smile. "It will serve you well."

I took it, feeling proud. My father was cooler than any make-believe superhero or spy.

As I walked him to the door, Papa said, "Miss Ida and Miss Lucille will stay with you until your mother gets home, okay?"

I wrinkled my nose but ducked my head when Papa narrowed his eyes at me. I resisted the urge to ask how the cranky twins were involved with this veil and the war they talked about. "Maya, listen to me," he said, his tone serious. "If you ever see the Lord of Shadows again in your dreams, run and find a place to hide."

"But what can he do in a dream?" I asked.

"He can kill," Papa answered, his voice grave.

EIGHT

ALL BULLIES ARE NOT CREATED EQUAL

MAMA GROUNDED ME for two weeks, which was generous, considering that I broke the rules twice. I didn't complain when she handed down my sentence after a lengthy talking-to that I wouldn't soon forget. It could've been much worse. Eli's grandmother was a yeller. Frankie's moms argued with statistics and facts, but my parents used *the Voice* (trademark).

We didn't talk about Papa's work, or about the veil or the darkbringers. Instead, Mama reminded me that even without the Dark, our world was dangerous. She cited the crime rate, robberies, gangs, drugs. People on TV talked about the South Side like we were on another planet. They didn't care that Chicago was more than skyscrapers and shopping and deep-dish pizza. That the people who lived in my neighborhood were no different from them. Now that I thought about it, our neighborhood rarely saw any trouble before the werehyenas. That couldn't have been by accident —we had the cranky twins on patrol, but there had to be more to it.

I reread all my volumes of *Oya: Warrior Goddess* while grounded, but even they couldn't take my mind off Papa. I searched the pages for mention of the mythological creatures from his stories. They were all there: the werehyenas, the kishi, the impundulu. But also Bigfoot, the bogeyman, and the abominable snowman. I'd always thought that Papa had got the ideas for his stories from the comics. We used to read them together when I was little. Now that I was over the initial shock, I had a thousand and one questions for Papa, starting with where and what was the *Dark?* I tried to keep my mind busy, but I couldn't help but worry, especially now I knew how dangerous his work was. I couldn't help but feel a little mad at him, too. How could he and Mama keep a secret this big from me? Me not telling my parents about the world turning gray was bad, but them hiding a *whole world* from me was even worse. I understood that they wanted to protect me, but I wasn't a little kid anymore. I could handle the truth.

After school ended for the summer, Mama let me go

outside to meet my friends for the first time in weeks. I jetted down the porch steps with Papa's staff in tow, to where Frankie was waiting for me.

"I thought your mother would never let you out," she said as we headed for Eli's house.

"I can't believe it either," I said, dodging a stray basketball from a group of older kids playing on the sidewalk. "How did your moms take the news about your superpowers?"

Frankie winced as she adjusted her glasses. "They went with my original theory that someone slipped something in the pudding at school, so they think we hallucinated the whole thing. And since I haven't been able to make the light come again, I can't prove them wrong."

"Maybe it only happens when you're scared," I said. "Like for self-defense."

Frankie rubbed her chin. "I'm definitely fine with not being scared again anytime soon."

An ice cream truck cruised down the streets with music playing over the loudspeakers. But even ice cream couldn't cheer me up. I wanted Papa home. We passed the snow cone stand and an elotes cart. The sweet smell of roasted corn and butter and chili made my stomach growl. It was hot outside, and people sat in folding chairs on their porches or perched on cushions on their cement steps.

When we reached Eli's house, Nana was tending to a row of cabbages in the garden. Jayla rode Eli's back as he weaved between tomato vines. Every year the garden had exactly seven different vegetables—Nana's favorite number.

"More killer robots at twelve o'clock," Eli proclaimed to his sister.

Jayla grinned, and her brushy ponytail bounced as she held on to his neck. "Run faster!"

For a grandmother, Nana didn't have a wrinkle in sight, even though her hair was completely gray. She wore it in braids that ringed around her head like a crown. "Well, if it isn't the night owls," she said, grimacing at Papa's staff. She looked like she wanted to snatch it from my hands. "I hope you've learned your lesson."

My face felt hot as I squeezed the staff tighter. "Yes, ma'am."

"Can Eli come to the park?" Frankie asked. "We promise to behave."

Jayla wriggled off Eli's back and ran over to Nana, almost crushing a cabbage underfoot. "I want to play in the dirt too!"

"Back before dark." Nana cut her eyes at Eli. "We have the bingo championship tonight."

"Oh, I won't miss it." He grinned. "I bet on old man Lucas."

"You bet against me?" Nana scowled. "Your own grandma."

"But you never win, Nana," Jayla chipped in, her face serious.

Nana murmured something under her breath as Jayla plopped down beside her.

"Any more news?" I asked Eli on the way to the park.

He'd been gathering stories of other weird things happening in the neighborhood. "No other werehyena sightings," he said. "I'm still mad that I didn't get to see them."

I bit my lip, hoping the werehyenas weren't stalking another neighborhood. Frankie and I got lucky because of her magic. If not for that, we would've been dog meat. I really wanted to tell them about Papa, but I didn't know if I should, since he'd kept this guardian thing secret even from me. I swallowed and held my words inside for now.

"A sinkhole formed in Mrs. Wallace's backyard this morning." Eli frowned. "But nothing strange outside of that. Totally not fair how boring it's been."

Both Frankie and I gave him a scathing look. Werehyenas threatening to eat you and writhing shadows were far from boring. After that, we needed all the boring we could get.

"What?" Eli shrugged. "You got to see something cool." Then he rolled his eyes at Frankie, a goofy look on his face. "She even has powers, she's a magical *being* now."

I thought about how the leader of the werehyenas had called us godlings and wondered what it meant. Was it like being a god, but not? Like a pretend god?

"I haven't been able to replicate the light or the force

from that night," Frankie said, brows scrunched into a frown. "So it doesn't matter."

"*Replicate.*" Eli shook his head. "Stop with your fancy talk, just say you can't do it."

Frankie glanced at her feet. Like me, she hated failing at anything. "I'm glad you were around to see it happen, Maya. Or else no one would believe me. Miss Ida and Miss Lucille told my moms that I have a *vivid imagination.*"

"Ugh, I hate when adults say that." I winced. "It's the worst."

It was almost noon by the time we got to the park. A bunch of kids were on the playground and more on the soccer field. Some adults walked around the track. Other families set up barbecue grills and picnic blankets. An older kid who looked like he was in high school brushed by Eli on his way to the soccer field.

"Fiend!" Eli called after him. "Can't you see we're having an important conversation?"

The kid flipped Eli the finger over his shoulder.

"I get the feeling that no one else knows about the weird stuff happening because of Miss Ida and Miss Lucille," I said. The cranky twins had tried to convince Frankie's moms that nothing happened, but why? Were they protecting Papa's secret about the veil too? "It's like they're doing damage control."

"Maybe they're possessed by evil spirits," Eli offered.

"One day they'll try to turn us into zombies, and we'll have to spray them with ketchup to snap them out of their trance."

My mouth fell open, and I blinked at Eli. "That's your most ridiculous theory yet."

"More ridiculous than the spiders in tiny tap shoes?" Eli asked, quirking an eyebrow.

"Definitely," Frankie and I both said.

"The ketchup made it over the top," Frankie said, her nose turned up in disgust.

"It should be paintballs," I said. "It'll be more fun too."

"Well, well," said a snarling voice from behind me. "What do we have here?"

I spun around to see Winston, the wannabe rapper/basketball star from science class. He was taller than Frankie, who was the tallest of the three of us. But instead of being lanky, he was big, with an even bigger attitude. He had a low 'fro with a lining so precise that it looked tattooed along the top of his forehead. Per his usual style, he wore a blue Golden State jersey (number 30) — he never seemed to run out of new clothes either.

He was with his cronies, Tay and Candace, two more clueless bullies who always messed with other kids. Tay had his hair in alternating red and black cornrows and wore a dozen gold chains around his neck. Candace was both a chess whiz and queen of the *deadliest* death stare at school. She held the record for making the most kids pee their pants.

Currently standing at forty-seven, including those who had done so more than once.

There was something different about them that I couldn't put my finger on. On the surface they looked the same. Their eyes burned with their usual mischief like they were hungry for trouble. But there was an extra layer of malice on their faces. Not like they just wanted to bully us —like they wanted to do much worse. I straightened up, my eyes sharp. I wasn't about to take crap from them, especially after standing up to the werehyenas.

Before I could say anything, Eli spoke up. "Winston, you were brilliant in the final quarter against the Raptors. I can't believe you hit that three-pointer at the buzzer."

Frankie and I flashed each other a look, and I swallowed a snicker. Winston was an awful basketball player and a terrible rapper. He had videos on YouTube, but only his friends followed his channel.

"Shut up, little godling," Winston said.

That word again: *godling*. That was not something Winston would say.

Candace pounded her fists together. "Let's teach them a lesson for being half-breeds."

"That's an offensive term." Frankie scorned her. "You should know better than to use it."

"Who is beanstalk talking to?" Candace asked, casting a glance at her friends.

I glared at them. "Why don't you guys get lost."

"You snot-nose godlings don't have any idea who you're dealing with." Winston gritted his teeth. "You think because you scared away a couple of werehyenas you're tough now?"

I shivered at the thought that he and his friends had been out that night too and done nothing to help Frankie and me. Not that I expected bullies like them to ever do the right thing. The fact that they knew about the werehyenas didn't sound like Winston and his crew either.

"Are you talking about those chicken werehyenas who tucked their tails and ran?" I asked.

"Are you kidding me?" Eli interjected, his voice high-pitched. "You've seen the werehyenas too? How could a bunch of losers like you get to—"

Eli cut off midsentence. He probably shouldn't have said that *losers* part out loud.

"I meant losers in the most endearing way," Eli blurted out through a half-sorry, half-goofy grin.

"It's time to put an end to these parasites," Winston said, stepping closer.

"Fight, fight, fight," someone else yelled.

In some neighborhoods when kids yelled *fight,* people gathered around to see the carnage. In other neighborhoods, people ran because fights meant someone could die. The people in our neighborhood split right down the middle. Half ran and half stood around to watch.

"Now would be a good time to use your powers," Eli whispered to Frankie.

"I already told you I can't," she shot back.

Winston charged first, and I sprang to action. With Papa's staff, I blocked his path. Something happened then that I didn't expect. The staff started to glow, and a warm tingling shot up my arm. The glowing shocked the bullies too because they froze for a moment. Papa didn't tell me that the staff had magic, but that must have been why he wanted me to keep it. To protect myself.

"You better leave before you get your butts kicked," I said in my meanest voice.

Winston and his cronies laughed. Them laughing like cackling hens only made me madder. Papa always said, *Never strike unless absolutely necessary.* I thought it was necessary to wipe that smug look from Winston's face, but I held myself back. That turned out to be a mistake. Winston shoved me in the chest so hard that I almost lost my balance.

I twirled the staff fast and hit him across his knuckles. He yelped and drew his hand back, but I wasn't done with him. Not by a long shot. I pivoted forward on my right leg to distract him as I thrust the staff into the soft part of his left shoulder. I didn't hit him with my full force

—just enough to warn him that he was messing with the wrong girl. Winston stumbled back, and I pushed down a grin.

He growled at me through clenched teeth and threw a punch so fast that I barely ducked out of the way in time. Then there were flying fists and screaming and bodies rushing at us. I knocked Winston and Candace on their butts, but more kids joined the fight. Kids who never got in trouble. Priyanka shoved Frankie to the ground. Tay came to finish the job, but Eli rammed his shoulder into the bigger boy and knocked him aside. Janae tried to lock me up from behind, and I rammed my elbow into her stomach.

Before we knew it, we were fending off more and more kids. No one was acting like themselves, and even with Papa's staff, I got kicked and punched more times than I cared to admit. Eli and Frankie weren't faring any better.

We knocked them down, and they kept getting back up. The magic in Papa's staff didn't do much more than glow. A dozen kids surrounded us, and Frankie, Eli, and I stood back-to-back. None of this made sense. These weren't kids who hung out together, let alone fought side by side.

"This is highly illogical, you know," Frankie said, half out of breath.

"Ha!" Eli laughed. "You both thought my ghost possession story was impossible."

"Who are you?" I demanded.

One by one, their skin faded from tan, brown, and black to cerulean, cobalt, and azure. The deepest blues and purples. They grew long, curved horns and barbed tails.

My heart slammed against my ribs, and the staff vibrated in my hands. These were not kids from our class. They weren't kids at all.

"Time for you to die, godlings," the one who had looked like Winston only a moment ago said, now in a voice as slippery as a snake. "Then we'll take your bodies back to our master."

Darkbringers.

As soon as the thought hit me, the sky darkened, and storm clouds settled over the park. There was no time for a snappy comeback as they closed in. Frankie's power hadn't shown, but she and Eli didn't back down either.

I attacked again with the staff, batting away barbed tails that stung when they tore into my skin. I couldn't worry about that now. I'd never fought against anyone but Papa, and there were a dozen darkbringers at our throats. I had to pay attention so I didn't hit one of my friends by mistake. I slammed the staff into shoulders, chests, and ribs to keep them back.

The darkbringer who had pretended to be Winston stepped away from the others and raised his arms. To my utter dismay, he sprouted the largest pair of wings I'd ever seen. Wings that were a shade lighter than his violet face and stretched over knotted bones. I didn't have time to be shocked for long before he took to the sky and the rest of the darkbringers followed his lead. He whipped his tail around as fast as lightning, and the barb sliced deep into my hand. I yelped and dropped the staff. Triumphant, the fake Winston smiled, then he dove headfirst, straight for me.

NINE

I SEE MY LIFE FLASH BEFORE MY EYES

B Y SOME STROKE OF LUCK, I leaped out of the way in time to dodge the fake Winston's attack. He was fast, but I was a fraction of a second faster. When I ducked, his claws raked across empty air instead of my throat. I was glad for that, but this was no time to celebrate. Winston halted midair and turned around, his wings beating hard. We stared each other down, then I glanced at Papa's staff at my feet. Winston gave me a conniving smile, daring me to go for it. I cracked my knuckles to distract him, and it worked. As soon as he looked at my hands, I lunged for the staff. The wood felt warm and comforting in my hands again.

Winston grimaced, and his eyes were full of pure hate.

But before he could attack, a loud screech rang out that shook the ground. I almost lost my balance, and my friends stumbled too. A sudden gush of hot wind swept through the park. It reminded me of the first night the shadows attacked me.

"I don't like the sound of that," Frankie shouted, looking around for the trouble.

But the answer wasn't around us; it was above. I glanced up to see a vortex of clouds and swirling indigo opening in the sky. It formed a wind tunnel that sucked up all the air, and the darkbringers were caught directly in its path.

"What the . . ." Eli said as the darkbringers tried to flee.

My friends and I backed away before we got caught in it too. This was something straight out of my comic books. In volume 62, Oya created a storm that sucked up the nuclear weapons on Dr. Z's secret island and sent them into space. This would've been exciting, had it not looked like an angry tornado about to destroy everything in its path.

A giant bird made of blue light circled the edges of the vortex. It was fast—too fast, enough to make my head spin. From what I could tell, *it* was causing the disturbance. Some of the darkbringers tried to escape, but it was no use. One clung to a stop sign with her feet and tail whipping desperately against the wind. Another one held on to a fire hydrant. The three who had pretended to be Winston, Candace, and Tay hugged a park bench for dear life. One by one the wind plucked them up. I could feel its pull on me too, until Frankie dragged me to the tree that she and Eli had ducked behind. The lightning bird rounded up the darkbringers like cattle.

Eli had whipped out his cellphone and was recording the whole thing. Once the last darkbringer disappeared into the vortex, the hole closed. Then the bird swooped down from the sky and landed on the ground in front of us. It stood ten feet tall, and its wings were huge. Now that it was closer, we could see that it was made of swiveling mist that never stopped moving. I wondered if it had come back to finish what the darkbringers started.

"If you were planning to take a selfie," Frankie said to Eli, "right now would be good."

"In trouble again, I see, Maya," said a disembodied gruff voice that floated from the light. A voice I'd heard so many times fussing at kids for stepping on her grass. The light shrank to the size of a human and turned solid.

One half of the cranky Johnston twins stood in front of us. Miss Lucille's pink bonnet sat too far to one side, and her white hair poked from underneath it. Her eyes blazed with the last of the blue light before she blinked and they turned normal again. Scratch that: the blue was *normal,* and the human face was her cover.

I crossed my shaking arms. If Miss Lucille was what I thought, then that explained a lot.

"Are you kids okay?" she asked, winded, looking us over.

"Are *you?*" Eli replied, tilting his head to the side. "You were just a swirling blue light."

Miss Lucille rolled her eyes and shook her head at him. But Eli was too busy angling his phone while he and Frankie posed for a selfie with her in the background. There was still a bit of the blue light around the outline of her body.

"You're an orisha, aren't you?" I asked, pointedly.

"Like from your comics?" Frankie frowned. "That's—"

Eli laughed. "Better than your genetic experiment theory."

Miss Lucille didn't answer my question, but she didn't deny it either. My cranky neighbors were *orishas*. The guardians of the universe. *They were . . . gods?* I gaped at her in shock.

"Come with me," Miss Lucille said. "It isn't safe here."

"Are there more of these darkbringers?" I peered around. The park was empty now.

"Come," Miss Lucille said again, and we didn't protest as we followed her.

When we reached my street, I saw Mama pacing back and forth in front of our house. She pulled me into a hug. Her tears wet the top of my head as she inhaled a shaky breath.

"I'm okay, Mama." She was treating me like a little kid, and in front of my friends at that.

"Let me get the first-aid kit," Mama said, looking over the three of us. We all had bruises and cuts. My T-shirt was ruined, too.

Miss Lucille stepped closer to me. "There's no need."

She tapped my forehead, and a tingling feeling spread across my skin. Within seconds, my injuries healed. She did the same to Frankie and Eli.

"How did you do that?" I asked, amazed.

"We have a lot to talk about, Maya," Mama said. "You three come inside. Miss Ida is on her way to get your grandmother, Eli, and we need to tell your moms, Frankie."

If Mama knew about the orishas, then Papa wasn't just the guardian of the veil, he was . . . I couldn't wrap my mind around it. I felt giddy and scared, but also I couldn't help but feel like my life had flipped upside down. There was another world out there hidden from plain sight, and I wanted to know everything about it.

My friends and I exchanged glances as we climbed up the steps to my house. Frankie fiddled with her glasses, and Eli bounced on his toes with excitement. None of us said a word as we plopped down on the couch in the living room. I was still in shock.

Mama paced back and forth again while Miss Lucille

peered out the window like she was looking for more trouble.

"I'm not sure how to tell you this, Maya, but your father isn't like other people," Mama said finally when she stopped pacing. She wrapped her arms around her shoulders. "Neither is Eli's grandmother, or Frankie's first mom."

When Mama said *first mom*, Frankie's back went rigid. Before she came to live in our neighborhood with her new moms, she had another mom. Her biological mother died in an accident when Frankie was little. She once told me that she remembered her mother's voice, which sounded like sunshine. She remembered the warmth of her brown skin and her smile, too.

"What about *her?*" Frankie asked, and I felt a flutter of heat in my belly.

"She was very special, dear," Mama answered. "She was a spirit goddess."

Frankie's lips trembled as she said, "Oh."

"You mean, *oh snap!*" Eli interrupted. "You're a goddess!"

I blinked once, then twice. "Frankie is an orisha?"

"It's a little more complicated than that," Mama said. "Her mother was an orisha, and her father was human. She's half orisha like you, Maya."

"A godling," I mused, finally figuring out what the word meant. The werehyenas and darkbringers called us that . . .

They called *us* godlings with an *s*. My mouth fell open when I realized what Mama had said. "Half orisha like me?"

"Eddy—Papa—is an orisha too, Maya," she said, searching my face for a reaction. Even if I figured it out before she told me—it was still overwhelming. If my father was an orisha like Oya, then did that mean she was real too?

Wait. Let me try that again.

My father was an orisha—a spirit god, a celestial, and *not* human. That thing I said about being overwhelmed—well, I might've understated that a bit.

"Your father's old name is Elegguá," Miss Lucille added.

"Elegguá," I said, trying the name out. "Why didn't you tell me before?" I'd already heard Papa's side of the story, now I wanted to hear it from Mama, too.

She wrapped her arms around her shoulders, her face worried again. "Eddy was trying to protect us from his enemies—those who would harm us to hurt him. But I see that not telling you was a mistake."

I remembered the man from my dreams again. The Lord of Shadows. He had smiled at me and shaken his head while his purple and black ribbons drained the color from the world. *Some people never learn,* he'd said. He was talking about Papa. "He's protecting us from the Lord of Shadows."

Miss Lucille drew in a sharp breath that she held before

exhaling. "There's a lot to cover, but your father and the Lord of Shadows have a long history," she said, stepping away from the window. "To understand, we have to start at the beginning."

"The beginning of what?" I had another bad feeling.

"The beginning of the beginning." Miss Lucille sat down in Papa's recliner. "The universe started as a vast blank slate. It existed without space, time, mass, or depth. It was endless and boundless and void. No one can say how long it remained that way before becoming aware, but soon after, it grew restless. Once the first sparks of matter and antimatter cropped up, the universe found its purpose. It would create. The universe birthed planets, moons, comets, asteroids, black holes, and stars. The things it made hummed with energy, and in their song came the universe's first and oldest name, Olodumare."

"You're talking about the Big Bang theory, aren't you?" Frankie said, frowning.

I was speechless as the news tangled in my mind. My head throbbed, and I massaged my temples. This was like taking a history class in five minutes. It was hard not to question everything I knew about my family, my neighborhood, even myself. But I soaked it all in, piece by piece. Now that the darkbringers had entered our world, I needed to catch up fast.

"That's what you call it nowadays." Miss Lucille

shrugged. "The first orishas, Obatala and Oduduwa, sprang from the universe. Together they created the darkbringers and gave them magic. But they didn't stop at that. They made hundreds of magical creatures from the microscopic to the gigantic, too. Obatala and Oduduwa left their creations for a time while they explored the vastness of the universe."

"Is that why the darkbringers can shapeshift . . . because they have magic?" I asked.

Miss Lucille nodded. "The Lord of Shadows, who lurked in the shadow of a planet, took the darkbringers under his charge while the orishas were away. He was one of the first celestials that the universe created, older than the orishas and time itself. He helped the darkbringers to develop at an accelerated rate. But the universe had already seeded life on earth in the form of what would become humans. The darkbringers consumed the resources from the ocean meant to sustain the seeds. Without that sustenance, the seeds couldn't grow, and many died by the masses.

"Once the darkbringers could survive on their own, the Lord of Shadows went back to the shadow of a planet and slept for a long time. While he was sleeping, other orishas were born and began to understand the nature of the universe too. The darkbringers flourished during that time, but the seeds of humankind suffered greatly. Obatala and Oduduwa saw that the seeds wouldn't develop if the orishas didn't intervene. They asked your father for a solution that would let the darkbringers and the new life coexist. He wove a veil upon the earth separating it into two worlds. That way, the seeds had a chance to evolve into something more than sea slugs."

Frankie frowned again. "Well, this supports the idea that humans came from sea creatures five hundred forty million years ago."

Eli waved his hand. "Sea *slugs*, not just any creature. Get it right."

All three of us—Frankie, Eli, and me—listened in disbelief. Frankie looked like she wanted to ask a thousand questions. Eli bounced on his seat, as if he was bursting with questions too. Papa was almost as old as the universe, and I couldn't wrap my mind around that. His driver's license said that he was thirty-nine, and I'd thought *that* was really old.

"The orishas didn't grasp how fragile life was back then," Miss Lucille said. "When your father wove the veil, it helped the humans evolve, but the darkbringers suffered. The sudden shift killed off almost all the crops in their world, since some plants couldn't survive in the constant dusk. Those darkbringers who weren't close to other food sources died. As immortal beings, the orishas didn't understand death at first."

She was dancing around the truth, but I understood

what she was hinting at. "You mean some darkbringers died because of what Papa did?"

"Millions died, Maya, but it was truly an accident," Miss Lucille said, glancing to her hands. "When the Lord of Shadows woke again and saw his people suffering, he waged war on the orishas. He was more powerful than they could ever imagine. He could absorb energy from others and drain the life from anything he touched.

"The war between him and the orishas lasted for centuries, until they found a way to negate his powers. Unable to kill him, your father trapped the Lord of Shadows in the Dark with the darkbringers. Eventually Eshu, the orisha of balance, created equilibrium between the two worlds. Life flourished in both. For a time, all was well, but the Lord of Shadows found a way to escape. He invaded a godling's dream and convinced her to open one of the ancient gateways. When he escaped, he killed Elegguá's family."

"His family?" I asked, my palms sweaty. "*We're* his family."

Papa never said he had a family. Mama's family lived in Georgia, and we only got to see them once a year during the holidays, but Papa said he was an only child. Come to think of it, he always avoided the topic of his parents, and now I knew why. He had none, not in the way we thought of parents. The universe was his father and his mother.

"The orishas are old as time itself. Many have had families over the millennia," Miss Lucille explained. "But Elegguá only ever had one family before . . . an aziza wife and their three children."

I could hardly believe what she was saying. *Papa had another family.*

"That was a millennium ago," Mama said, picking up the story. "When the Lord of Shadows escaped the Dark, he killed them out of revenge." Mama's voice faded, as if she didn't have the strength to say more.

Although the cranky twins looked older than Papa, it turned out they were only two thousand years old, give or take a decade. They were also godlings like us. After what happened to Papa's first wife and children, they vowed to help protect his family. I took a deep breath. It sucked feeling like you were the last one to know everything.

"The orishas imprisoned the Lord of Shadows in the Dark again," Miss Lucille continued. "After that, your father swore that he'd never have another family. He went centuries living a life of solitude until he met your mother."

"He never hid who he was, Maya," Mama said. "It wasn't easy for us in the beginning, but we moved here so you could always be safe. There's an orisha community like this one on every continent."

My friends looked as overwhelmed as me. "Are all god-lings half human and half orisha?"

"Godling means *part* orisha," Miss Lucille corrected. "Nana Buruku came up with the term *godling* three or four millennia ago. As long as you have a drop of celestial DNA, if you can call it that, then you're a godling. Doesn't matter if you're one-half or one-eighth. The orishas claim all their offspring."

"Nana's an orisha?" Eli gasped, his eyes shiny with surprise. "Who else is one?"

"Your highly respected grandmother is head of the orisha council that oversees this community." Miss Lucille wrinkled her nose at him. "At the start of the first war with the Lord of Shadows, there had been four hundred and one orishas. He killed a third of them before Elegguá was able to trap him in the Dark. Over the millennia, their numbers dwindled to one hundred seventy-two, almost all due to the second war. So we don't repeat the mistakes of the past, some of them have stepped in to set rules for how we interact with mortals. That is how communities and councils came to be. As for who else is an orisha, that is not my place to say."

Dwindled was a nicer way to say that they had died. It was hard to believe that one celestial being was powerful enough to kill so many immortals. Also, I didn't miss that she'd said *almost all due to the second war,* which meant that orishas had died from other causes too, including Frankie's mom. "Outside of a few, most humans don't know orishas exist, do they?"

"Correct," Miss Lucille said. "The orishas decided that the magical species must keep themselves hidden from humans. Among them are the aziza, woodland fairies wary of outsiders. The elokos, who are forest-dwelling elves with an insatiable appetite. There are also the trickster kishi, with their two faces, and the adze, who are fireflies that feed on blood. And of course, the werehyenas, who, as you've seen, can be unpredictable. There are countless more. It's the orishas' job to keep magic from interfering with human development, as the universe intended."

"How is it possible that no one knows?" Eli waved his phone. "I got video. No way no one else in the world hasn't already uploaded video to YouTube. Somebody's seen something."

"*Do* you have video?" Miss Lucille said, raising an eyebrow.

Frankie and I hunched in close to Eli as he played the video. It was completely blank.

"Magic doesn't abide by human-world rules," Miss Lucille said.

"But if we've seen magic, can't other humans see it too?"

I asked. "And what about the human parents in our neigh-borhood—don't they know?"

Miss Lucille went on to explain that a third of the children in our neighborhood were godlings. The orishas had made a pact to not tell their human families the truth unless one of the godlings showed powers. Until Frankie, none had for hundreds of years.

"My sister and I can alter reality," Miss Lucille said. "If a human happens to see or come upon magic, we make them think it was something ordinary. It's not very hard, since they struggle with the concept of magic to start." Miss Lucille sighed as she looked us over, her own face showing something bordering on pity. "I know this is a lot to take in, but Eleggguá thought it best to fill you in on the basics before he returned to go into the details. Now that the veil is failing, everything has changed."

Frankie's powers were cool. I wanted to be like her, like Oya, like Papa. I had the staff, but it wasn't the same as hav-ing magic of my own.

"There's a lot more to tell you," Mama said. "But you've heard enough for—"

We all jumped when there was a knock on the door. Miss Lucille sprang to her feet—nothing old about the way she moved now. She sure didn't have any problems kicking those darkbringers butts in the park either. Both she and

Mama rushed to the door, and Miss Ida burst into the room. Sweat dripped down her forehead.

"What's wrong?" her sister demanded.

"I got word from Eshu," Miss Ida said, half out of breath. "He was with Elegguá patching up a large tear in the veil." Her face was grim and flustered. "The Lord of Shadows ambushed them . . . Eshu got away, but Elegguá . . ." Her pained eyes landed on me when she said, "He's gone. The Lord of Shadows took him into the Dark."

TEN

MY WORLD FALLS APART

A MAN MADE OF THE SCARIEST NIGHTMARES had taken Papa into the Dark. I squeezed the staff so hard that my fingers ached. Even though Miss Ida's words echoed in my head, I swallowed down my tears. Papa needed me to be strong.

Mama held her emotions behind a stern face, her shoulders squared, her chin tilted up. "Eddy will find a way to escape," she said, her eyes defiant. "He always comes home."

I wondered if every time Papa left, she worried that something like this might happen. Was that why they had hidden the truth from me?

"We have to get him back!" I yelled.

"It's not that easy, Maya." Miss Lucille winced. "Don't you think we'd go if we could? Your father created the veil so that no one could cross between worlds. That's the whole point of it. There are protocols and procedures we must follow."

"I don't understand," I said, itching to do something. "The darkbringers came here."

"They came through the tears in the veil," Miss Lucille explained.

"But you said there were protocols and procedures you must follow," Frankie said. "Does that mean there is another way?"

Miss Lucille crossed her arms. "I've said all that I'm going to. It's up to the orisha council now. Elegguá's instructions were clear if something happened to him."

"Which were what, exactly?" I let out a frustrated breath that would've gotten me a warning under normal circumstances. "My father wouldn't want you to do nothing."

"Keep you and your mother safe," Miss Lucille said, her face hard. She wouldn't budge.

"There are three ways to enter the Dark," Miss Ida chimed in, casting her sister a sidelong glance. "*One*, through a rip in the veil. *Two*, through one of the ancient gateways. Or *three*, by opening a portal, which only Elegguá can do. But none of that will matter if the veil completely fails."

I bit my lip, my mind reeling. We needed to stop wasting time and do something now. "Why can't we use one of the ancient gateways to rescue Papa?"

"There's no *we*, Maya," Mama snapped at me. "You'll stay put in *this* house."

"Mama, I'm not going to hide while—"

I stopped midsentence as Mama went completely still. Her mouth was half open, but no words came out. She looked like my math teacher, Ms. Vanderbilt, when the world turned gray before. *Frozen like a mannequin.* The grandfather clock stopped ticking. Both Frankie and Eli bolted to their feet, their faces twisted in a mix of fear and surprise.

Miss Lucille cursed under her breath, then said, "It's happening more and more."

"What . . . what's happening?" I asked, choking back tears. "What's wrong with Mama?"

"She's going to be fine, Maya." Miss Ida patted me on the shoulder. "Time falls out of sync when there is a rip in the veil nearby. We're not immune, but humans are more sensitive to its effects."

"How is that possible?" Frankie said, taking a careful step closer to Mama.

Miss Lucille raised her hands so that her palms faced each other with a gap between them. "The veil isn't a flat surface," she explained. "My left hand represents the human world, and my right hand represents the Dark. The space between my hands is the veil. Try to think of it as a barrier between the two worlds that exists outside of space and time."

"Wait a minute," Frankie said, drawing out each word as the hands on the grandfather clock started to spin backwards. She had *that* look again. "So, when a place *with time* intersects with a place *without time,* time temporarily goes haywire. Almost like how the gravitational pull of a black hole slows time down."

"Speaking of which," Eli groaned. "This is not the *time* to be frankiefying us with science . . . this is serious."

"I am being serious." Frankie scowled at him.

Before they started arguing, I asked, "How are these tears happening?"

"There have always been normal tears over the years because the veil is so old," Miss Lucille said. "But there've been bigger ones lately and too often. The council suspects . . ."

Mama drew in a gulp of air that startled us. When her eyes landed on my friends, she glanced at where they had been sitting on the couch before time got messed up. "How did you get over here?"

"Well—" I started to explain when a scream from outside cut me off.

No, not *a* scream. A lot of people screaming.

Miss Lucille and Miss Ida were the first to get to the window. They became a blur of blue light around the edges, moving faster than anything that should be possible. No wonder Frankie and I had lost track of them the night the werehyenas attacked us. Frankie, Eli, and I crowded behind them. Frankie gasped, and Eli pressed his face and hands against the windowpane. My heart slammed in my chest at what I saw outside.

A streak of crooked black lightning cut through the air near a green Camry across the street. The space around it rippled like a rock hitting water. When the edges of the black lightning begin to expand, I realized that we were seeing a tear forming in the veil. As it grew bigger, the car fluctuated like a mirage and shifted to make room for the black hole at the center of the tear. It was the weirdest thing I'd ever seen — even weirder than the werehyenas. Nothing disappeared or got crushed, there was just . . . more space. The Camry still sat next to the hole.

"Incredible," Eli whispered, his jaw dropping.

Black ink bled across the sky, and it looked like we were in the early hours of night instead of the middle of the day. But none of the streetlights came on. I held my breath when the hole stopped growing. It was now massive enough to fit an elephant. Light sparked around the edges, but the center was dark. It was like looking into the belly of a murky well and not quite seeing the bottom of it. I could make out a sea of dark faces in the shadows. Without warning, something shot out of the hole and slammed into the oak tree in front of our house. Splintered bark and pulp burst into the air, and we stumbled away from the window.

"Stay here!" Miss Lucille shouted. Before I could protest, she and her sister became mist and melted through the wall, as if changing their physical form was as easy as putting on a new T-shirt. As soon as they left, Eli jetted from the window and out the door.

"I have to make sure Jayla's okay," he yelled. "She was in the yard playing."

"Eli, wait," Mama said, running after him.

Frankie and I ran close behind her, and I had Papa's staff.

Outside was complete chaos. People I'd known my whole life tried to free themselves from writhing shadows. My ex-babysitter, Lakesha, dodged a shadow only to have another one rope around her ankle. She fell down, and LJ, her cousin, stomped the shadow over and over until it let her go. He helped her up, and they ran away.

They were the lucky ones. Some shadows wrapped people in cocoons and dragged them toward the tear in the veil — toward the Dark. I thought of the night the shadows had almost gotten me too — how scared I'd been. I couldn't let this happen in my neighborhood.

Eli was out of sight by the time Mama made it down the

porch steps and ran into a dark mass that stepped into her path. She stumbled back, her head tilting up slowly as my mind struggled against reality. The darkbringer standing in front of her was seven feet tall and as wide as a pro wrestler. When he breathed, steam came out of his nose like smoke from a chimney. His two curled bull horns were the color of blood. Looking down at Mama, he smiled, revealing pointed teeth. His razor-sharp, barbed tail whipped around in a flash, cutting through the air, aimed straight for her.

"No!" I leaped down the steps, spinning the staff. Mama needed my help. Before the darkbringer knew what hit him, I cracked the staff against his tail. He fell back, howling in pain. Mama backed away too and almost tripped over me, but Frankie grabbed her arm.

"Maya, watch out," Mama yelled.

I barely ducked out of the way as the darkbringer's claws swiped within striking distance of my face. Going on the offense, I angled the staff up and slammed it into his chest. A burst of light came from Papa's staff, and the impact sent the darkbringer hurtling through the air.

I gasped, finally understanding why my hands and arms were tingling. The staff had done more than just glow. It had real magic. Was that why the Lord of Shadows and his darkbringers were able to trap Papa? Because he didn't have his staff to defend himself?

My heart thundered loud in my ears as I took in my

neighborhood. More darkbringers came through the black hole next to the Camry. They were three times the size of the bullies on the playground and ten times meaner-looking. They wore dark uniforms—like soldiers, but they didn't have any weapons. The one who had attacked Mama joined his friends in the center of the street. I counted seven of them.

White flashes of light swept down from the sky. Two landed in front of the darkbringers. They hadn't moved at all, as if they were expecting this. The rest of the light swept through the neighborhood and freed people from the shadows.

I bit my lip, hoping that Eli found his sister. I didn't think these darkbringers cared if they hurt adults or kids.

One of the white lights in front of the darkbringers dimmed. Eli's grandmother appeared in its place with her hands on her hips. It was Nana but also *not* Nana. She was taller, wider, and her brown skin sparked with light. Her braided white hair glowed too. She wore a purple dress with black tights that rustled in the wind. The cranky twins said that Nana was an important orisha, but I never imagined that she'd be so . . . *divine.*

Beside Nana, the other light shaped itself into our science teacher, Mr. Jenkins. Frankie gasped. He was her favorite teacher, after all, and we didn't have a clue that he was an orisha too. Lightning sparked across his brown skin and flecks of gold covered his cornrows. He had twin axes across his back, and he wore a red tunic. In my comics, an orisha who looked like him had helped Oya stop a zombie apocalypse.

"Mr. Jenkins is *Shangó?*" I glanced up at Mama. "The orisha of thunder and lightning."

She nodded, her eyes still glued on the darkbringers.

"You should have stayed on your side of the veil," Nana said, her voice younger. She raised her hands, and the ground shook. Roots sprouted up from the patches of grass along the sidewalks. At first they looked like worms poking their heads from the dirt, then they shot out into the street. They twined together and formed bars around the darkbringers so they couldn't escape.

"We come with a message," one of the darkbringers hissed. It was the one who attacked Mama. The one who looked like the blue Hulk.

I swallowed hard, again thinking of the Lord of Shadows. The cranky twins said that he took long naps. Maybe he did that to regenerate after digesting all the life he drained from the world. Had he been asleep before the tears started in the veil again? Was he somehow causing them now?

"Go back to the heavens or die with your precious humans," the darkbringer growled.

I remembered then. The orishas were celestials who belonged to the universe, not a particular planet.

"You dare threaten us?" Nana demanded. The dark-bringers shuffled closer together as her vines thrashed at them. When I say vines, these were as thick as pythons and looked like they could crush every bone in your body.

The tear in the veil began to shrink. It was like Papa said. The veil was repairing itself. It made me wonder: if this was a *small* tear, then how big were the tears he had to mend that couldn't heal on their own? They must've been the size of whole cities or even larger. How many darkbringers could get into our world through them? I didn't want to do that math.

The shadows that had slithered out of the tear disappeared back into the hole. Nana had the darkbringers trapped. Some of them looked miserable as their way home started to vanish before their eyes.

"Where is Elegguá?" Mr. Jenkins asked, his voice like ice.

"You want him," the darkbringer said. "Come into the Dark and get him."

I tightened my hand around the staff and gritted my teeth.

"How are you tearing the veil?" Nana asked.

"Soon our master will be able to come here himself." The darkbringer ignored her question. "And he'll destroy this world without so much as lifting a finger."

"Too bad you won't live to see it," Nana said, her voice

echoing in my head like a drum. Her skin glowed brighter, and more vines joined the others. There were so many now that we couldn't see the darkbringers anymore. A bright light flashed, and I shielded my eyes. When the light faded, the vines and the darkbringers were gone.

"You girls wait here," Mama said. "I need to talk to Nana and Shangó."

Frankie and I glanced at each other, shaking to the bone. I clasped Papa's staff close to my side. There was no sign of the darkbringers or the vines.

"Did she send them back into the Dark?" Frankie whispered to me.

"That or wiped them from existence," I said, not sure I wanted to know the answer.

I couldn't let Papa stay in the Dark. The Lord of Shadows was dangerous and unpredictable. With Mama talking to the orishas, I inched toward the tear in the veil that was still open. It was a little taller than me now but shrinking fast. I stepped closer, my chest heaving up and down.

"Maya, what are you doing?" Frankie asked, grabbing my arm.

"I'm going after Papa," I said. "He needs his staff."

Frankie frowned. "I don't think that's a good idea."

"I know, but I'm going," I said as she let go.

Fat tears filled her eyes. "What if something happens to you?"

"It'll be okay," I said, glancing at my feet. I couldn't bear to see her so scared for me, but I had to do this for Papa. I ran across the street, and as I reached the black hole, I felt the energy from it vibrating against my face. I took one step in, and someone jerked me back.

I tried to wriggle away, but the person twirled me around. I looked up at a bushy white beard. It was Ernest, the man who always sat in front of the corner store playing his harmonica. He'd been missing from his spot for weeks now. Fire burned in his eyes—real flames where his pupils should be.

"Maya, what were you thinking?" Miss Lucille appeared next to him. "Thank the universe you were here, Eshu."

Eshu, the orisha of balance—the one who was with my father when the Lord of Shadows took him. He stared down at me with a twinkle in his eyes, and I noticed for the first time that he looked a little like Papa.

"You're not going anywhere, future *guardian,*" he said in a deep voice. "We need you."

I watched desperately as the tear in the veil closed—crushing my chance to help Papa.

Eleven

When something ordinary becomes magical

"Maya Janine Abeola!" Mama yelled. "Have you lost your good sense?"

Mama and the orishas were staring at me like I was the worst kid in the world while I brushed tears from my cheeks. I didn't care that I was going to be in trouble again. All I could think about was how the tear in the veil had disappeared before my eyes. "That was our chance to go after Papa," I said, my shoulders slumping. "We had a way in, and now it's gone."

"Maya." Miss Lucille took a placating tone like she was talking to a little kid. "Do you think a twelve-year-old can just walk into the Dark and come out in one piece?"

Eshu drew a finger across his throat so I'd know how

dangerous it was. Nana shook her head and pursed her lips to show her disapproval. I got that the grownups were trying to keep me safe, but it was hard to think about my own life with Papa trapped in the Dark.

"Ernest . . . I mean, Eshu," I said, my voice shy. Seeing his harmonica on a red and black cord around his neck now made me think that just maybe things could be normal again. We would get Papa back. "You called me 'future guardian.' What does that mean?"

"It doesn't mean anything *yet*," Nana answered for him.

I winced and bit my lip. "What do you mean by *yet?*"

Shangó and Eshu glanced at each other, and I couldn't read their expressions.

The *yet* part really worried me. Papa was guardian of the veil, but did that mean I would become guardian if something bad happened to him?

"I mean that you're still too young, Maya," Nana said, her voice gentler.

Eshu flashed me a reassuring smile. "And your father will have to train you."

"But how can I become a guardian if I don't have any magic of my own?" I said under my breath.

"That's not for you to worry about now, little one," Shangó said as the axes across his back vanished.

Right before our eyes, the three orishas changed into

their human forms. Nana appeared older. Lightning stopped sparking across Shangó's skin. The fire burned out of Eshu's eyes. Now they stood in front of me looking as normal as ever. My mind tried to convince me that everything that happened was my imagination, but I wasn't fooled.

Eli ran down the sidewalk with Jayla bouncing on his hip. Nana met them halfway and pulled them both into a hug.

"I saw the night monsters, Nana!" Jayla said excitedly as she climbed into her grandmother's arms.

"Not monsters, sweetie, people," Nana said, glancing to Mama. "Please come down to the community center with the children after the twins clean up this mess. I'll assemble the rest of the council. There is much to discuss."

Mama gave the orisha a wary nod but said nothing.

At that, Nana, Mr. Jenkins (Shangó), and Ernest (Eshu) set off toward the community center. Jayla waved at Eli, who stayed behind, scratching his head.

"Are you sure Nana's an orisha?" Eli cocked an eyebrow at Miss Lucille.

With Miss Lucille looking sour, Frankie whispered, "You missed all the real action."

"Ultimate facepalm." Eli slapped his forehead. "I always miss the fun stuff."

Soon the dark clouds lifted, and it was bright outside

again. Miss Lucille glanced up at the sky. "Whenever the darkbringers come into our world, they bring a bit of the Dark with them."

Every single neighbor on my block was in their front yard or on the street. Some were taking pictures of the hole in the oak tree or the torn-up grass where Nana's vines had burst from the ground. Some were in shock and couldn't stop shaking. Miss Ida moved to stand apart from the rest of us. Swirling blue smoke curled between her fingers.

"What is she doing?" Frankie asked, and I thought I knew.

Miss Ida raised her hands up and blew across her palms. The blue smoke stretched into long tendrils that swept through the crowd. A warm breeze tickled my arms as the magic passed over me while it seemed to linger on my neighbors' skin.

Now that the commotion had died down, my ex-babysitter Lakesha and her cousin LJ had come back and were standing in front of her house. She stared down at her phone. "I had video of everything. I swear I did."

"Did you remember to hit Record?" LJ rolled his eyes. She *was* good at forgetting things. Like the time she was babysitting me and left the popcorn on the stove too long. Or when she let her hedgehog out of his cage and forgot to put him back in. She found him two days later at the bottom of a laundry basket, gnawing one of her socks.

When the magic on the wind hit her, her face went blank. So did LJ's.

"What's happening?" another neighbor standing on his porch asked.

As my neighbors' faces went blank one by one, I turned to Miss Lucille. Her eyes glowed with blue light again. "Is Miss Ida doing what I think?"

"She's making them forget," Miss Lucille confirmed.

"Are you going to steal our memories too?" I backed away. I wouldn't let the cranky twins make me forget that Papa was in trouble.

"Of course not, Maya." Miss Lucille flicked her wrist and the hole in the tree disappeared and the ground went back to normal. When she was done, no one had so much as a dirt spot on their clothes to remind them of what happened. "My sister's directing her magic at the humans only . . . It's better that way so they're not afraid."

Frankie crossed her arms. "You can't just do something like that. It's not right."

"Totally not cool to mess with people's minds," Eli said, wagging his finger.

"I don't have time to explain it again." Miss Lucille frowned. "We're finished here, and we need to get you to the orisha council."

Finally.

Nana and the other orishas must have a plan to get my father back.

My heart pounded against my chest as we walked down Wood Street. Everything looked normal, except people from another dimension had attacked our neighborhood twice. And orishas — real orishas — pretending to be humans had saved the day. No one outside of my friends and Mama would even remember it.

Every muscle in my body was wound tight. Papa was missing, and I couldn't accept that he was really gone. *Was he . . .* No, he wasn't. He couldn't be. I wouldn't let myself think it.

As we walked block after block, Frankie and Eli kept trying to reassure me that everything was going to be okay. But their words echoed in my head as my eyes stayed on my father's black staff. It was easier to focus on it so I didn't burst into tears. The white symbols engraved in the staff reflected in the sunlight. *I am the guardian of the veil.* That was my father's job, but Eshu, the god of balance, had called me *future guardian.* If things were different, that would've been exciting news, but right now I just wanted Papa back.

When we reached the community center, I sucked in a deep breath. Even from the sidewalk, you could smell the chlorine from the swimming pool inside. Older kids played basketball in the gated courts next to the center. There was a playground too, where most of the younger kids liked to hang out. A gardener knelt in the flower bed in front of the building tending to a rosebush.

Everything about the two-story building looked plain. Weather had worn down the red bricks, and mold filled the gaps between the concrete. The windows were frosted so you couldn't see inside, but it wasn't anything special. I never in a million years would've guessed that gods had made *this* place their headquarters.

Miss Lucille led the way inside the community center. The reception area had dingy tan walls and black-and-white-checkered tiles. I always thought the place looked like something straight out of another century. The girl at the receptionist's desk, Carla, wore blue glasses that matched her lipstick. She glanced up from her cellphone, her face bored, until her eyes landed on the cranky twins.

"Miss Ida and Miss Lucille." She nodded at them, then looked at Mama, me, and my friends like she was unsure if she should say more. "The *council members* are expecting you."

Miss Ida smiled, but I could tell her mind was someplace else. "We're ready."

Carla snapped her fingers. "You may pass."

Frankie, Eli, and I shrugged, not sure why she snapped her fingers. But Mama and the cranky twins said nothing as they headed for the metal detector. Miss Lucille entered first and disappeared. I stopped in my tracks, and Eli ran straight into me. Frankie stopped too, her eyes wide with glee.

"I never knew magic could be this cool," she said, after a big gulp.

"Totally unfair that Nana never told me about this," Eli said, sulking.

I guessed that he was feeling the same as me. I was still struggling to catch up when the rules of the world kept changing. But I wouldn't let the fear of the unknown or uncertainty stand in my way of rescuing Papa.

"Totally unfair," I agreed as Miss Ida disappeared next.

The mechanics of the metal detector were fascinating. Nothing out of the ordinary *seemed* to happen when the grownups passed through it. No loud shriek like when Miss Lucille had raced to the park in her spirit form. No bright light like when Frankie created her force field. Or warm tingle against my skin like when Miss Ida made our neighbors forget the darkbringers. Yet, they had vanished into thin air. Clara snapping her fingers must've opened some sort of portal.

On the other side of the metal detector, I could see down the hall into the main room. There was a small stage with round tables where Nana hosted bingo every Monday, Thursday, and Saturday night.

Had I not seen the cranky twins disappear, I wouldn't have believed the metal detector was a gateway. Where would it take us? Mama gave me an encouraging smile, then walked through it herself.

"Here goes nothing!" Eli said, racing in front of Frankie and me.

"No running indoors!" Carla yelled, but it was too late. Eli vanished.

"You're next," I said to Frankie, giving her a fist bump before she disappeared through the metal detector too.

"You're his kid, aren't you?" Carla asked, leaning forward over her desk.

We both knew who *he* was.

"Elegguá will be okay, you know?" She paused, her eyes turning more serious. "He's never failed us before, even when the Lord of Shadows . . . when he . . . well, you know."

When the Lord of Shadows killed my father's first wife and children.

"I know he won't," I said, my voice firm. "He's the guardian of the veil."

I walked through the metal detector, knowing that there was no turning back. After today, my life would never be the same. I was completely unprepared for what happened next. My body lurched forward like I was on a roller coaster without a padded bar to keep me from falling. For a split second, I couldn't breathe, and my heart raced. The elastic band holding my locs in a ponytail popped, and my hair flew across my face.

I bit back a scream as a gust of wind lifted me from my feet and flung me down a long hall. I flew through the air at a breakneck pace, not slowing even when a speck of light appeared ahead of me.

The golden light grew bigger the closer I got. Soon I realized it was an archway above a pair of gilded double doors and I was about to slam right into it.

"Somebody . . . anybody, help!" I yelled, but there was no one to hear me. "Please!"

Racing toward the doors at the speed of light, I squeezed my eyes shut and braced for certain death.

TWELVE

IN WHICH I MAKE A DECISION

SHEER TERROR SEIZED MY MIND as I hurtled closer to becoming a human pancake. My life didn't flash before my eyes, but I did almost pee my pants. I forced myself to open my eyes. If I was going to die, I was going to face death head-on. Besides, there *was* something exciting about flying for the first time.

I wasn't spinning wildly through the air. I felt an invisible walkway of air beneath my feet as solid as a real floor. Magic glued me to it and kept me from falling. I didn't see either of my friends splattered on the black marble floor below, which was a good sign.

When I was inches away from impact, I clenched my teeth, convinced that my life was over, but I drew to a sudden stop. Magic held me suspended in the air in front of the golden doors. Doors that could only be for giants or gods who liked to prance around in giant form. They were at least three stories tall and as wide as the Willis Tower. Up close, I could see symbols engraved in them. Stars, planets, plants, animals, and objects. Some were like the symbols on Papa's staff, but many I didn't recognize.

"What are you doing hanging around up there?" Eli shouted from below me.

"Just taking in the scenery," I yelled back at the top of his head.

"We don't have all day, you know," he said, tapping his foot.

As if the magic had been eavesdropping on our conversation, it lowered me toward the floor. I had to admit descending in an invisible elevator would've been cool under better circumstances. When my feet finally landed on the black marble, my legs felt like jelly.

Eli beamed. "That was almost as great as riding Goliath at Six Flags Great America."

"Yeah, right, *almost*," I said, forcing myself to laugh when I was still shaking.

Frankie poked her head through a crack between the doors wide enough to fit a baby giraffe. "What's taking you both so long? Everyone's waiting."

"Brace yourself," Eli said, winking at me. "You're not going to believe this."

That turned out to be an understatement. I took one step beyond the doors and almost collapsed. I inhaled a sharp breath—surprised that I could breathe at all. Eli was right. My mind struggled to make sense of what I was seeing. "Whoa," I whispered, soaking up the impossible and improbable nature of the moment.

I jumped a little when the doors behind me slammed shut and disappeared. Taking a step forward, I wondered if anyone would fault me if I picked now as the time to freak out. There were no walls, but we stood in a chamber with four pillars for support, one in each corner, smack in the middle of outer space.

Not to shout, but:

OUTER SPACE.

Mental note: don't go near the edges; no guardrails.

Thousands of fireflies buzzed around the ceiling and lit the open chamber in a soft light. The stars near the pillars where the floor ended and space began were humongous, while the ones farther away looked like grains of sand. A comet streaked by so close that it rattled my teeth.

Once I was over the initial shock, I saw Frankie's moms, Pam and Dee, standing next to Mama in the center of the empty chamber. The cranky twins were here too, but there was no sign of Nana and the orisha council.

"Do you still think this is an illusion?" Dee was saying to her wife.

Pam, the taller of the two, wore a tweed jacket and jeans. Dee had on high-top sneakers and her white lab coat. When you looked at Frankie and her moms together, you couldn't tell she was adopted. The three of them wore similar black-rimmed glasses and had genius hair. Think Albert Einstein's hair, except kinky.

"This could be an elaborate holograph," Pam answered, narrowing her eyes at the cranky twins. Between the metal detector and here, they had removed their pink bonnets. Both had their silvery hair pulled back into braids that flowed down their shoulders.

"I assure you that it is not," Miss Lucille said, wrinkling her nose.

Frankie squeezed between her moms, who each wrapped an arm around her. Mama gave me a sad smile as she pulled me into a side hug.

Eli cupped his hands around his mouth and called, "Nana, where are you?"

"Eli!" Jayla's voice rang out from somewhere. "We can play with the stars!"

"Calm yourself, girl," came Nana's voice, shushing her.

"Jayla's here?" Eli protested. "How long has she known?"

"*Now* is not the time, Eli," Frankie whispered to him, her face smug with revenge.

Clusters of stars swiveled around the chamber like mini dust clouds. Each sparkled and glowed a different color. A yellow one there. A pink one here. A green one that touched the tip of my nose as it floated by and left my face vibrating. Imagine that someone shrank solar systems and put them in a bottle. This was like being in the bottle with them if the bottle was big enough to fit eight people.

A light flashed in front of us, and high-back golden thrones shimmered into existence. The council members sat on them in their semidivine state. I remembered the orishas from my comic books—but seeing them like this was exciting and a little scary. They were gigantic, and we were specks of dust next to them.

To the far left sat Shangó, aka Mr. Jenkins, his double axes at his feet, lightning flickering against his skin. He was the orisha of thunder and lightning. Protector of innocence, hardest science teacher at Jackson Middle School. He was known for his strength, but sometimes he got distracted by his curiosity.

Next to him sat Eshu with fire burning in his eyes again. Better known in our neighborhood as Ernest, the Blues Man. He was the orisha of balance, who caused the earth to spin to create day and night and the seasons. But he was also sometimes a trickster.

Nicknamed the grandmother of the orishas because of her wise nature, Nana Buruku sat next to him. Her brown skin shimmered with soft light. She embodied the spirit of earth and all things that supported life, but she hated metal. It weakened her powers. Jayla was sitting on her lap until she spotted Eli and climbed down. She ran to him, and he scooped her up in his arms and spun her around once while she clung to his neck.

Nana shrugged. "She wouldn't stay with the sitter."

Miss Mae from the beauty salon sat next to Nana. She also ran the shelter on Forty-Seventh street that helped people who'd fallen on bad luck get back on their feet. I bit my lip trying to figure out her orisha name. She wore a beautiful yellow dress that lapped at her bare feet like a flowing river. The five gold rings around her neck sparked with stars, and her pretty braids lay across her shoulders.

"You're Oshun," I blurted out. "The orisha of beauty."

"Among many other things," said Oshun smiling at me, and when she did, her face glowed like the first morning sunrays. Eli's jaw dropped open, and Frankie rolled her eyes at him. "Stop embarrassing us," she said, under her breath.

I remembered from my comics that the orishas had many responsibilities. Oshun represented fresh water, love, prosperity, and fertility in addition to beauty. Next to her sat our crossing guard at school, Zane, in a green shirt that seemed to blend in with his throne. His dog, General, was at his feet. Both man and dog wore matching shimmering metal tags. General had changed too. He had six eyes instead of two and three times as many teeth.

"Ogun." I looked at Zane. "The orisha of metal and war."

Nana turned her nose up like she smelled something foul.

"At your service, *little one*," Ogun answered, tipping his head to me.

Eshu said something to Nana in a language that made the room shake.

"Is that Parseltongue?" Frankie nudged up her glasses.

Pam shook her head. "That sounds nothing like Parseltongue."

"I bet we're going on a quest," Eli whispered to me. "Demigods always got quests, so godlings must too."

We were the equivalent of demigods, like Hercules or Achilles or Perseus. But from the looks of disapproval on the orishas' faces, we were not at the top of their chosen heroes list. "Doubt it," I murmured.

Eshu's eyes burned with fire as he regarded us, then he said, "Welcome to the gods' realm. We brought you here because it's easier to show you who we are than explain. By now, you know that the guardian—Elegguá—has been taken—"

"Are you going after him?" Mama spoke up, her impatient voice echoing in the chamber.

"That's a complicated question," Eshu answered, his fire dimming a little.

"What's so complicated about it?" I thrust out my father's staff. "We have to help Papa."

"I know this is hard to understand right now, Maya, but we must be careful." Nana sat forward on her red-and-gold throne. "The Lord of Shadows is very dangerous. If he was able to hurt Eshu and kidnap Elegguá, then that means he has grown powerful again. No one from any of the councils can risk leaving their family unprotected right now. He'll come after our children to exact revenge against us. The godlings wouldn't stand a chance. Except for a very few, most haven't shown any gifts in a millennium."

I frowned. "How could he grow more powerful if he's trapped in the Dark?"

Miss Ida spoke up. "Your father discovered that the Lord of Shadows has found a way to tap into the energy of the veil." She stood as still as a statue and didn't look like she was even breathing. "He's absorbing it."

That got everyone's attention, including mine.

"So he's using the veil like a battery?" Frankie grimaced. "That's clever."

Eli sighed, shaking his head. "She means well . . . She's just a little socially awkward."

"You said very few godlings have shown powers in

generations." I squeezed the staff tighter. "But Frankie used magic against the werehyenas."

"Yes, she's one of the few." Nana nodded at Miss Ida and Miss Lucille. "After the twins here."

Frankie straightened her glasses. "Does that mean human genes are dominant and orisha genes are recessive?"

"No, but good guess, Miss Williams," Shangó answered, his voice more like our science teacher's now. "If we were at school, I'd give you extra credit."

Frankie beamed as he added, "The orisha gene grows dominant only when provoked."

We all stared at him, wondering what he was talking about. "If there's something that awakens it," he clarified. "One by one, godlings who had no magic abilities started to show the signs right before the second war with the Dark a thousand years ago. The universe has a way of giving us what we need. The godlings helped us push back the darkbringers after the Lord of Shadows convinced a foolish child to open one of the gateways. That said, even then some of the godlings never showed powers and died in battle."

"Then we should go after Papa now," I demanded. "Before it's too late and the Lord of Shadows drains the veil completely."

"We can't just waltz into the Dark," Oshun said, her voice as sweet as music. "We made an oath to Olodumare to protect humankind after our earlier grave mistakes." She clutched at the gold rings around her neck, staring into space (literally). "It's much too dangerous for us too . . . You don't know what it was like before. The Lord of Shadows possesses the power to destroy only in the way the universe can. Our very existence is at risk."

"Fortunately, your father designed the veil so that the Lord of Shadows can't cross even if there's a tear," Nana added. "The universe only knows the trouble we would be in if he could slip in through a crack."

"What if we use one of the ancient gateways and catch him by surprise?" I asked, desperate. It wasn't that I didn't understand what the orishas were saying, but it didn't change my mind. "I can get Papa back if you're too afraid to go."

"Be careful of your vanity, young guardian," Oshun said, stroking her elaborate necklace. "Believe me, as the most beautiful of all the orishas, I know much about vanity and the trouble that it can lead to. Your father has been training you in the ways of the staff against our better judgment." Then she leaned forward, her eyes narrowed and her chin tilted up. "But do not think yourself so accomplished that you can do what gods cannot."

"I know—" I started to say, but Oshun shushed me, her voice an off-key musical note.

She studied her pink nails. "You don't know enough to know what you don't know."

Her haute couture, beauty queen act was starting to get on my last nerve. So what if I didn't know everything? I knew that Papa was in trouble and this conversation was a waste of time.

"To answer your question." Nana sighed, her face looking tired even in her semidivine form. "While the veil still stands, the gateways are the only way the Lord of Shadows can enter our world. He didn't even know they existed until he befriended a godling in her dreams and tricked her into using a key to open one. She paid for her mistake with her life." She turned to the twins and blew out a deep breath. "I trust that you haven't let any other details slip?"

"No, Nana," Miss Lucille said, her eyes on her feet. It was weird seeing Miss Ida and Miss Lucille so defeated. They were the toughest old ladies in the neighborhood.

My heart dropped in my chest. "You are going after him, aren't you?"

"We have called to our brethren at the edges of the universe to assist," Nana said, resigned. "Even orishas can't travel the breadth of Olodumare in a day, but once they're here, we will go into the Dark after your father. For now, we must ensure the veil remains intact. If it fails, the Lord of

Shadows will stop at nothing to destroy the human world
and our children who are bound to it. We must protect
them first."

"I can't believe this," I said through clenched teeth. I
was so mad that my whole body shook. "Every second that
we waste talking, Papa could be . . . he could . . ." But I
couldn't finish my sentence when I saw the anguish on
Mama's face and the shine of tears in her eyes. I wouldn't let
the Lord of Shadows destroy my family. I would find one of
the ancient gateways without the orishas' help and get Papa
back.

Thirteen

What dreams are made of

MORE TEARS CROPPED UP in the veil over the next few days, but no darkbringers came through the holes. Their presence had been a warning and a challenge. The warning: an army waited on the other side in the Dark. One that was way more dangerous than the darkbringers sent to rough up my neighborhood. The challenge: come look for Elegguá if you had the guts to face the Lord of Shadows.

You want him, the darkbringer had said. *Come into the Dark and get him.*

Mama took off work to stay home with me. While the whole neighborhood celebrated the Fourth of July, we waited for news that never came. We spent day and night pacing back and forth, staring out the window. Still nothing.

None of the other orishas had the magic to heal the fissures in the veil. If a large tear opened that couldn't heal itself, more darkbringers could enter our world. The orishas and cranky twins worked nonstop to follow the tears in the veil just in case. But there were too many, and they couldn't be everywhere at once.

After a week off work, Mama's rotten boss (my words this time) said either she had to come back or he'd find someone to replace her. That night Miss Ida came over to watch me while Mama went to work. After the council meeting, neither twin would spill about the gateways.

If Papa's stories were real, then he must've mentioned the gateways in them. Something the cranky twins said stood out too. There was an orisha council on every continent to guard their offspring and humans. What if they were also guarding the ancient gateways? If so, then each orisha community would likely be close to one. *But where?*

Frustrated that I didn't have an answer, I climbed into bed and curled up on my side. My eyes landed on the Comic-Con tickets on my nightstand. For the first time ever, I couldn't have cared less about going to the convention. It didn't matter anymore; nothing mattered while my father was still in danger. If only I had my own powers, then maybe I could open a gateway into the Dark myself. I could do anything other than sit around and wait for news. That was the worst part — waiting and not knowing. I pulled the blanket up to my neck and sank low in my pillow. Although my mind was racing, I fell asleep and entered a dream unlike any other.

In the dream, I was standing in front of my house again when a slippery voice said, "This is my place, little girl, or should I call you *Maya?*"

A chill crept down my back as I whipped around fast to see the Lord of Shadows floating at the end of my street. It was the middle of the day and the sun was high in the sky, but the space where he hovered was as dark as night. His purple and black ribbons writhed like snakes around him.

"I never thought Elegguá would be foolish enough to take another wife," he added with a devious smile. "Do you know what happened to his first wife and their three children? Kimala, Genu, and Eleni . . ." His violet eyes grew wide with excitement. "I took them away from him. I took everything that he loved the same way he tried to destroy everything I loved when he created the veil."

"You're a murderer!" I yelled, tears choking in my throat.

"I am so much more than that," the Lord of Shadows said, drawing out each word. "I'm a liberator."

Anger welled up inside me. He had some nerve talking about liberation, as if I didn't know what the word meant. He'd done the right thing long ago when he helped the darkbringers. But after Eshu balanced the light and the dark and the darkbringers were well, he went too far. He let his need for revenge turn him into a monster.

"Tell me where my father is," I demanded.

He laughed. "Why would I make it easy for you?"

I gritted my teeth, wishing I had Papa's staff to show him a thing or two.

The Lord of Shadows' many ribbons moved him forth as gracefully as a spider darted across pavement. His legs, if he had any, were hidden beneath curtains of darkness. I stumbled back, remembering what Papa said, his eyes grave and worried. *Maya, listen to me. If you ever see the Lord of Shadows again in your dreams, run and find a place to hide.*

I wanted to run, but I wanted answers too.

I glanced at my feet, not sure how to find my father on my own. That was when I saw the Comic-Con tickets sticking out of my shirt pocket. The event started in a few days. I remembered something else Papa said before he left. *By the time we go to Comic-Con, you'll understand everything.* Why were the tickets *here* in this dream? Was my subconscious mind trying to give me a clue? The answer was *literally* right under my nose.

"Comic-Con!" I blurted out, then slapped a hand over my mouth before I said too much. I couldn't risk the Lord of Shadows finding out the location of one of the ancient gateways.

The Lord of Shadows smiled, eyes bright with mischief. "You seem like a strange little thing . . . nothing like Elegguá's previous children, but I'm afraid that won't save you."

I bit back a curse. I couldn't believe this jerk. He was taunting me and disrespecting the memory of my half siblings in the same breath.

The Lord of Shadows slithered toward me on his bed of wriggling ribbons. But no matter how hard he tried to come closer, the distance between us only grew wider. My left hand tingled. When I stared down at it, Papa's staff shimmered out of thin air and lay in my palm. The wood was blacker than night, and the white symbols swirled like dancing rings of fire. The sun, a leopard with raised paws, and a river. *I am the guardian of the veil.*

There was another message that stood out: a leopard with raised paws with two crosses and a circle. *I am the master of the crossroads.* This wasn't a dream but the place where *our* world intersected with the Dark. Not a gateway like what might be at Comic-Con, but a place where only gods could exist.

My eyes went wide as two things occurred to me at once. First, the Lord of Shadows was a god too. A terrible one, but one no less. He was a celestial being like the orishas. Second, I was at the crossroads because I was a godling, which would be great if I had inherited some of my father's magic. I understood something else about the crossroads, too. It had magic of its own, and that was how the Lord of Shadows was able to use it to invade my dreams.

The magic had reached into my mind and read my desperate plea to keep the Lord of Shadows away. That was why the street kept stretching between us. It stretched because I *needed* it to keep me safe.

"You're a fast learner, Maya." The Lord of Shadows' smile finally faded. His face looked as pale and fragile as a porcelain doll. "The orishas avoid the crossroads, but you . . . you're different. You're like your father in ways yet to be discovered. Another fly for me to swat."

Mama always said that people had moral compasses. That deep down they knew the difference between right and wrong. I wasn't sure how anyone's moral compass worked. And I thought that maybe one person's compass was different from the next person's. From the evil gleam in the Lord of Shadows' eyes, I didn't think he had a moral compass at all.

His threats made my heart race, but I had my father's staff, and the magic in it grew brighter. Power radiated in my palms, climbed up my arms, and spread through my body. If the staff had magic and the crossroads had magic, then I could use both to my advantage. I whirled the staff in front of me, creating an arch of white light. It shot out toward the Lord of Shadows and stopped him in his tracks.

The light turned into vertical bars made of glowing crystals that trapped him in a prison.

I *almost* exhaled a sigh of relief, until the Lord of Shadows laughed. His voice echoed in the crossroads and the pavement shook beneath my feet. He reached one long, crooked finger to touch a crystal bar. It dissolved into a fine powder that sprinkled the ground.

"You're as arrogant as Elegguá too," he said. "He has done you a disservice by hiding the truth. A good father would have prepared you for your death."

"And you would know what makes a good father?" I huffed. He had no right to say those things about Papa. He was wrong. Papa was a good dad. Better than good. My father was the best. He did what he could to protect me and Mama, even if it meant working tirelessly to keep the veil from failing. Now I understood why Papa said that no one else could do his job, and the incredible burden on his shoulders. I could feel a sliver of that burden too.

"Where is my father?" I demanded again, my jaw set.

The Lord of Shadows' expression was unreadable when he said, "He's at the epicenter of where it all began for *you*."

I didn't understand, but maybe that was exactly what he wanted. This was some sort of sick game for him. He wouldn't tell me outright.

The houses along the street started to peel away like

chips of old paint. The same thing happened to the trees, the cars, and the sidewalks, too. Like an artist had taken a scalpel to a canvas to scrape away the color. The pieces floated in the air until they disappeared, leaving nothing but a dusting of dark blue. It reminded me of the time between night and sunrise.

"A glimpse into the Dark," the Lord of Shadows said, spreading his arms wide. "Where you will die."

With one step forward, he was suddenly standing right in my face. It happened so fast that my heart dropped to my stomach. His ribbons snapped at me, and I batted them away with the staff. When the staff connected with the Lord of Shadows, magic jerked me back into the human world.

I bolted up in bed, gasping for air. My chest heaved up and down, and it took a minute to work out what happened. The Lord of Shadows had tried to kill me. My wrist burned where one of his ribbons had touched my arm. It happened on the crossroads, but the pain was real.

My eyes landed on Papa's staff propped against my bed, then the Comic-Con tickets on the nightstand. Both were pulsing with a soft blue light. That couldn't be a coincidence. The orishas said that the gateway into the Dark had to be opened with a key. What if it wasn't a literal key? It could be some kind of object.

The staff will serve you well, Papa had said, before he left for the Dark.

It hit me all at once. The staff was the key to opening the gateway.

FOURTEEN

Comic-Con, here I come

I MARKED THE CALENDAR, counting down the days to Comic-Con. When the time finally arrived, I snuck out of the house while Mama was still sleeping and met up with Eli and Frankie. It took two buses and two trains, but we got to the convention center in one piece. I stopped in my tracks in the parking lot, hardly able to believe my eyes. Hundreds of heroes and villains were filing into the arena. Characters from DC Comics, Marvel, and every popular cosplay under the sun. Dark knights. Rich billionaires with fancy gadgets. Homegrown country boys with secret super-human powers. Tyrants and fairies and robots and monsters. This place was everything I ever dreamt and then some.

I squealed (a little) when I saw four people walking

together all dressed as Oya: Warrior Goddess. One wore the outfit from volume 182. A purple head wrap, black catsuit, and rainbow boots. Another wore the yellow and green dress from that time she went undercover at an art gala.

"Maya." Eli snapped his fingers in front of my face. "You're drooling."

I couldn't believe this, not after years of begging Papa to come. But my excitement deflated fast. He should've been here with me — not missing, not in danger from some power-hungry monster. My chest ached every time I saw anyone who looked like him in the crowd. The man in the Black Panther costume. Or the one with the long locs dressed as Clark Kent or the tall Ichigo with deep brown skin and orange hair.

I clutched my backpack straps, determined to find the gateway. "Let's go."

Once we were inside the arena, the air smelled of popcorn and cotton candy and butter and ketchup. It made my stomach growl, even though I'd eaten breakfast. There were so many colors and lights that my brain almost short-circuited. People milled around on a floor that was so big you couldn't see from one end to the next. They stood in long lines to get autographs from their favorite characters. I took a deep breath. This was going to be much harder than I thought. I had no idea where the gateway to the Dark would be, and there was a lot of ground to cover.

"This place is awesome," Eli exclaimed. "Way more exciting than that paranormal con I went to last year."

"I'm getting a costume like that for Halloween," said Frankie, eyeing a group of warriors in red and black leather.

Eli cocked an eyebrow. "You, a *Dora Milaje?*"

"I don't need superpowers to kick your butt," Frankie said.

Eli was light-skinned, so you could see when he was embarrassed. His cheeks got pink like they were right now. He grinned as he scratched his head. "True."

While no one was looking, I whispered to the staff, "Can you show us the way into the Dark?" I had no reason to believe it would work, but if the staff were a key, then maybe it would have some connection to the gateway. I cringed when a kid in a marshmallow costume gave me the stink eye for talking to a stick.

The staff tugged my arm to the right, and before I knew it, we were on our way, navigating through the crowd. Ahead of us, some stormtroopers shoved a group of superheroes taking selfies out of their way. It figured that people dressed up as the most mindless villains ever would be so rude.

"It's leading us to that hallway over there." I pointed across the massive room at the corridor labeled B22–23.

"Umm, Maya." Eli tried to get my attention, but I was too focused on the staff to listen.

With so much shouting and shoving, it was hard to find a way through the crowd to the hallway.

"What the . . ." I started to say as I saw that the eight stormtroopers had lined up in front of me and my friends. They had blue barbed tails and horns poking from the top of their white helmets. "I didn't see *this* coming." When I said *this,* I meant the darkbringers dressed up in costumes or them at Comic-Con.

I swallowed hard as Frankie, Eli, and I backed away.

"That's what I was trying to tell you," Eli yelled over the noise.

"Those aren't stormtroopers, are they?" Frankie asked.

I glanced behind us, and luckily we weren't surrounded. "Most definitely darkbringers."

"Run or fight?" Eli asked.

"Run!" I yelled.

We ran all right, and the darkbringers ran after us. People screamed, and some laughed because they thought it was a practical joke. Magic sparked off Papa's staff in waves and struck innocent bystanders. It changed a girl's hair from black to hot pink, then turned popcorn into worms. It electrified the fake crows hanging from the ceiling and made them come to life. They pecked at each other's strings until they freed themselves. Finally realizing that this was no joke, the crowd broke into full chaos.

We were about to escape when meaner, bigger dark-bringers stepped into our path, cracking their knuckles. They wore the bright green jumpsuits of Dr. Z's cronies. I mean, come on. Of all the villains to choose from, they had to pick the worst of the worst.

Now that we were this close to the darkbringers, I noticed that some of them had pimples like teenagers. Take away the tails, the horns, and the blue hue of their skin and they were just big, mean bullies. It was less scary to think of them that way than as monsters from another dimension trying to kill us.

The cronies stepped aside, and I gasped when I saw Dr. Z himself strolling through their ranks. He was a lanky darkbringer with deep purple skin and a shaved head and dressed in a white suit. Even his lapels and cuffs shimmered with gold like the real Dr. Z's.

He smiled, revealing a mouth of sharp pointed teeth. "Godlings." His voice was at once squeaky and deep like how boys a bit older than us sounded sometimes. "I can smell you a mile away."

Eli sniffed his armpit and shrugged. "I forgot to put on deodorant again."

"Don't be silly." Frankie shoved her glasses up. "I'm guessing he smells our hormones, which must be different from normal humans. Maybe if we were orishas, full orishas, we could sniff them out too. Sort of like a calling card."

"They aren't exactly trying to hide," I said, staring at the fake Dr. Z.

"Hey, dude, who made your costume?" some guy in a hockey mask asked. He had a bemused face like he'd missed the memo that the rest of the con was in utter chaos.

The fake Dr. Z snarled as his tail lashed out. I blocked it with Papa's staff before he could strike the man in the hockey mask. That got the man's attention. Wide-eyed and scared, he ran away. The stormtroopers crept closer behind us. It was pretty clear that they were after us and no one else, which figured.

Dr. Z drew his tail back and wrinkled his nose at the people filing out of the exits. "Look at these fools. It will be easy to destroy this world once our armies come."

"Can we enjoy our time at Comic-Con until then?" I said, squinting at Frankie, then the closest exit. She nodded, catching on to my plan, and nudged Eli.

My answer only made Dr. Z angrier, and he waved for his cronies to attack. When they charged, I slammed the staff against the floor, and sparks of magic rippled out from it like waves. The magic knocked the darkbringers off balance but not off their feet. The light bulbs in the ceiling exploded and plunged the room into darkness. At which point, the emergency exit lights over the doors flared to life.

Everyone who hadn't had the sense to flee before caught a clue and ran for their lives.

"Go!" I yelled, and the three of us shot toward the closest exit too.

We ducked around scared and confused people and ran into an empty hallway. This one still had working lights, and we stopped to catch our breath.

"Those guys are really starting to get annoying," Eli said, winded.

Frankie wiped her forehead. "Not to be the bearer of bad news, but . . ."

Dr. Z and his cronies stepped into the hallway in front of us. And the stormtroopers blocked the double doors that we'd just come through.

"Time to finally die, godlings." Dr. Z laughed, and his laugh was diabolic, sure, but didn't have the true throaty timbre of a supervillain's. He had a ways to go.

"We're not afraid of you," I said as the staff tingled against my palm again.

Eli squeezed his fists tight. "If only I could call my ghost army."

"Huh?" I asked in the middle of trying to figure out what to do.

"When my powers do show, they'll be to call forth a ghost army," he said, completely sure of himself. "It's obvious with my love of the paranormal."

"So obvious," I said as the darkbringers charged.

Frankie pushed out blasts of power that knocked several of them on their butts. Staff in hand, I raced toward the remaining darkbringers before I lost my nerve.

Dr. Z whipped his tail around, the barbed end aimed straight for my heart, like a killer wielding a knife. I cracked my staff against it with all my strength. He screamed and jumped out of reach. "Don't just stand there!" he growled at his cronies. "Get them!"

I dodged darkbringers left and right, sweeping the staff along my body in a wide arc. I knocked down two who tried to double-team me. Then I pivoted right to distract another one, while swinging the staff left. I crushed hands and cracked ribs and jabbed the staff into bellies. The darkbringers may have looked invincible, but they fell like anyone else.

The sound of bones breaking made my stomach flip-flop, but I kept pushing. Hurting people for real wasn't something I wanted to do, but I had to protect us. I got my friends into this awful mess.

"Watch your back," Eli yelled as he ducked under my staff and rammed his shoulder into a darkbringer. He head-butted another one, and punched a third. Even if he didn't have magic, he was fast, and the darkbringers ran themselves in circles trying to catch him.

Frankie flung balls of light that knocked the darkbringers back one by one. They weren't like the werehyenas, who had tucked tail and run away. The darkbringers were smart, and some dodged her attack. Most of them didn't seem to have magic. I hadn't considered that some wouldn't, and I thought it must be like how most godlings didn't have magic either.

Dr. Z spread his fingertips, and two metal prods slipped out from underneath his sleeves. They looked like the batons that police wore at their hips but slimmer. Light shimmered off the bluish metal as he squeezed his hands around the handles. He swung both prods at once, and I swept the staff up to catch the blows. The metallic blue prods sent an electric shock up my arms. I stumbled back. Every muscle from my hands to my shoulders felt like jelly.

"Thanks to you, we know there's a gateway here," Dr. Z said, closing in on me again. "It's only a matter of time before we figure out how to open it." He squeezed the prods. "Instead of waiting for the veil to fail, we'll walk right through the front door and crush humankind."

I set my jaw, but I was shaking all over. I wanted to smack my palm against my forehead or bang my head against a wall. This was my fault. I mentioned Comic-Con in front of the Lord of Shadows. How could I be so dense? I had handed him the location of one of the gateways on a silver platter. Now people—no, not just people—*everyone* was in danger because of my careless statement. Like the veil failing wasn't already enough to worry about.

"Elegguá's *spawn*." The darkbringer smiled, then spat on the floor. "The Lord of Shadows will be pleased when I bring you back."

"Bring me back?" I glared at him. "Good luck with trying."

He gritted his teeth and struck again and again until the shock from the prods almost made my arms go numb. I tightened my grasp on the staff and willed it to absorb the shock instead of spreading it. The next time he attacked, the staff didn't vibrate. I laughed but regretted it when I caught a blow on my shoulder. Sharp pain shot down my spine, and I bit the inside of my cheek until I tasted blood. My knees shook.

But I couldn't let him win. I started to pay closer attention to his attacks. He always shifted his entire weight forward on his toes when he struck. Plus, he looked tired too.

Papa had given me plenty of lessons in staff fighting. One thing I always remembered was to stay nimble on my feet. The darkbringer must've missed that memo.

I danced around Dr. Z and cracked the staff against the upper part of his tail, breaking the bone. He yelped as he tried to elbow me, but I kept moving. His steps grew slower, and sweat streaked down his forehead. When he swung one of his prods, I hit his left hand and his weapon crashed to the floor. Then I rammed my staff into his stomach. When he bent over, that was the end of it. I knocked him out cold.

Eli scooped up the prods by the handles. "I'll take these off your hands."

Frankie and I knocked out the last of the darkbringers while Eli messed around with the prods. He pressed a button on the handles, and they stopped buzzing with electricity. We'd done it. We kicked darkbringer butts. But, well, they kicked our butts too.

I bit my lip and confessed to Eli and Frankie that I'd accidentally ratted out the location of the gateway. Then I told them about the cryptic clue from the Lord of Shadows. "He said that he took my father to the epicenter of where it all began for *me*."

"What does that mean?" Eli frowned. "Epicenter—like the center of an earthquake?"

"Maybe not so literal?" Frankie frowned too.

"I don't know, but we'll find out soon enough," I said, uneasy, then I whispered for the staff to take us to the gateway. It lit up, and a gentle force tugged me forward. We ran down empty corridors for what felt like forever. How could a building be so big? It didn't seem possible, but we finally made it to Hall B22–23.

We ended up in front of a door that said STAFF ONLY. Not waiting for my nerves to kick in, I snatched the door open and found mops, brooms, and a yellow bucket. Cleaning supplies. I had two overwhelming feelings. Excitement that we'd found the gateway into the Dark and disappointment because it was . . .

"The entry to the Dark is a broom closet?" Eli stuttered.

The only answer I could give him was the truth: "Yes."

FIFTEEN

CUE THE DARK

MAYBE PAPA'S STAFF got it wrong. A broom closet couldn't be the gateway into the Dark. But a cool breeze undercut the smell of bleach and vinegar that stung my nose. It came from behind a row of mop buckets against the back wall where we didn't see any vents.

I wrinkled my nose as I stepped inside. I thought about how the metal detector at the community center had transported us to outer space. Nothing happened in the closet except for me bumping into some spray bottles on the floor. When I inhaled again, I caught a hint of fresh grass and trees. This room was definitely more than it appeared. We just had to figure out how to get the gateway to open.

"Let's see what happens if we close the door," Frankie suggested.

She and Eli crowded into the room with me, and if not for the breeze, it would've gotten hot in there fast. With the door closed, it was completely dark, and I clumsily tried to find a light switch, without luck.

"Hey, watch your elbow," Eli said. It could've been mine or Frankie's. I couldn't say.

"Watch your knee, will you," I shot back.

"Maybe the light switch is outside the room," Frankie said.

"Give us light," I whispered to the staff. It glowed so bright that I squeezed my eyes shut. "Not so much." I winced, and the light dimmed to a soft glow.

"Ugh, that thing has a mind of its own," Eli said.

"I wish I could dissect it," Frankie added. "I'd love to see how magic works."

Eli laughed. "Not to sound too gross, but someone might say the same about you."

Only Frankie and Eli would get into an argument in a broom closet about dissecting a stick versus a person. While they argued, I turned over the staff in my hand. The magic hummed, and the symbols moved. It wasn't like when the sun hit the staff and they shimmered. This was different. They danced around the surface of the wood, and I could see them inside my head too — like I had double vision. The leopard, the tree, the lion, grass, sand, stars, suns. Too many symbols to keep up with. I thought about the crossroads and how there must be so many things I didn't understand. The orishas had kept a whole magical world a secret.

Without warning, I was suddenly in two places at once: in the closet with my friends and in the gods' realm. This wasn't the same place the orisha council had shown us with the minigalaxies. Instead, the white shimmering symbols from Papa's staff floated in the black space around me. I gasped when I saw no floor under my feet, but I didn't fall.

"Are you guys seeing this?" I asked.

"What . . . the symbols moving on the staff?" Eli said. "Um, yes."

"No, the gods' realm," I said as the symbols spun around me.

"Then no," Frankie said. "It must be a part of opening the gate."

In the gods' realm, I traced the complex symbols in the air with my fingers, drawing curves, loops, and circles. Sharp edges and angles and letters. The symbols glowed in golden light both there and in the closet on the staff. They spun around faster. I was afraid of what was happening but also excited. It wasn't every day you got to call forth magical symbols to open a gateway into another dimension.

My friends' voices rang in the back of my mind, but they sounded far away. Even when Eli snapped his fingers in front of my face, I couldn't stop. He was in the closet, but his hand somehow disturbed the symbols in the gods' realm. They exploded into showers of dazzling fireworks. But as soon as he moved his hand away, the symbols reformed before my eyes. Then I realized what I had done. I'd moved the symbols into an order that spelled out

I am the guardian of the veil.

Then the symbols—the sun, a leopard with raised paws, and a river—flew at me fast. This was the hardest part to understand. I could feel the symbols inside me—burning beneath my skin. They searched to see if I was the true guardian. I got the distinct feeling that if the symbols didn't like what they found, they would burn me to a crisp.

But soon the burning stopped. Did the symbols know I was the *true* guardian's daughter? Before they left to rejoin the others, they painted a complex walkway in my mind made of hundreds of symbols. That was how the gateway worked. I had to use the symbols to build a bridge to cross over into the Dark. I realized something else too—something that edged at the back of my mind. This space carved out in the gods' realm was a gateway to many dimensions that humans had no clue about. It didn't make sense for me to know this, but I could feel the vastness and the possibility of countless choices. The countless doors to countless worlds.

I rearranged the symbols at first into simple strings that got more complicated the more I added. They reminded me of a three-dimensional puzzle. The symbols twisted and bent and stretched to spell out a code. I didn't know if the order was right, but my subconscious mind seemed to understand the nature of the symbols. I wondered if this was how the Lord of Shadows tricked the godling into opening the gateway before. It was a chance I had to take. But to be safe, I adjusted the code by instinct, making it so that the gateway would close on the human side as soon as we entered it.

Fatigue quaked through my legs, and the symbols started to blur around the edges. I bit my bottom lip, trying to keep focused, but I was losing the pattern.

"No," I whispered as the gateway shrank. The magic was slipping from my grasp, and I struggled to keep it. "This can't be happening now."

Eli put a hand on my shoulder. "You okay?"

My legs shook, and a wave of dizziness washed over me. Of course, always at the worst time. I hadn't had an episode since the werehyenas. I sucked in a deep breath through my clenched teeth, but the dizzy spell only grew worse. In any other circumstances, I would've sat down. That was what

Mama and Dr. Kate always said. But I couldn't do that now. If I stopped building, the gateway might disappear completely. I couldn't let that happen.

"Her anemia," Frankie answered for me.

When my legs buckled a bit, she and Eli each wrapped one arm around my waist so I wouldn't fall down. A groan escaped my lips as the last symbols settled into place. The symbols would open the portal, but it wouldn't stay open long, so we had to go now.

The gods' realm disappeared, and the gateway opened at the back of the closet. It appeared as a six-foot spinning circle of gray rings that whipped out cold wind. This was the bridge I'd seen in my head.

"Whoa," Eli said.

We were at the point of no return. I hardened myself to the brisk breeze and clenched my jaw in defiance. Even if I had to crawl my way into the Dark, I would. There was nothing that would stop me from going.

"It's ready," I whispered, breathless, as the dizziness settled in for the long haul.

"Let's do this!" Eli said, his voice bright and eager. He really was way too excited after having faced darkbringers twice.

"We don't know what we'll find," I warned. "Be prepared for anything."

My friends stiffened next to me, and even the giddiness

faded from Eli's face. We didn't know if we'd end up in another broom closet in the Dark or the bottom of Lake Michigan. What if there was a darkbringer army waiting on the other side?

These and a thousand other thoughts went through my head as I stepped into the tunnel with my friends at my side. Our footfalls echoed as we walked on polished stone. The rings spun so fast that they vibrated our feet and up our legs. I wanted to reach out and touch them, to prove that this whole thing wasn't happening inside my head. On second thought they sort of reminded me of fan blades, and I rather liked my fingers on my hands.

We saw phantoms of ourselves moving outside of time, walking alongside us on the bridge. At one point, I leaned over and faced the ghost version of myself, who did the same. The cranky twins had said that time didn't exist in the veil. Now I suspected there was much more about this place and the other realms that defied science and logic.

"This is creepy," Eli said, swiping his hand through the phantom of himself, which made it dissipate. Moments later, the phantom reappeared, looking annoyed, and poked out his tongue at Eli.

Even though the portal stretched into a dark abyss, it only took a minute to get through the gateway. After a sudden jerk forward, the next thing I knew, we were a tangle of legs and arms and knees and elbows. We landed on the edge of a cornfield beneath a huge crooked tree with black leaves. Since we didn't have a darkbringer army bearing down on us, we had time to work out how to detangle ourselves. For a moment, I lay on my back, staring up at the dark sky. It was twilight, and the moon was only a shade or two lighter blue than the night.

The stars were dimmer here. I couldn't make out any of the constellations. Not the Little or Big Dipper, not Orion's Belt, or the North Star.

It was Frankie who sat up first and said, "The stars are reversed. The Big Dipper is pointing in the opposite direction. See . . ." She closed one eye and traced the constellation with her finger, and sure enough, she was right. It was all reversed, like the Dark was the opposite of our world. We'd left in the middle of day, and it was night here.

Finally, the dizziness passed, and I stood up. The grass rustled in the cool breeze.

"So far so good, eh?" I said to be cheerful, although we were too scared to move from our spot. The gateway had closed as soon as we hit the ground. I didn't think I could make another one for a while since I was so tired from building the first.

Eli grimaced as he raised his hands in front of his face. Yellow slime dripped down his arms. "What the heck . . ."

He cursed under his breath. In the tree above his head there was a half-destroyed bird's nest sprinkling down hay.

As soon as the words came from Eli's mouth, a bird as colorful and big as a peacock nosedived straight for us. But this was no peacock and definitely not dropping in to say hello. It shrieked with its talons stretched wide. I barely shoved Frankie out of the way in time.

"What is that?" Eli crouched with eyes pinned on the place where the bird skidded to a halt. "That's the biggest and fastest bird I've ever seen."

I knew exactly what kind of bird that was. An impundulu. It had eyes like shiny black marbles and an orange beak as spiked as barbed wire. Spines sharp enough to pick your teeth with jutted out like fish bones from its belly. Another one landed at our backs, the same hungry look in its dark eyes. Seeing an impundulu was a sign of bad luck. It meant that we would run into serious trouble on our journey, but this was much worse. When we came through the gateway, we'd knocked down their nest. Now Eli was wiping his hands on his pants with what was left of the impundulu's eggs.

I racked my brain to remember exactly what Papa had said about the impundulu.

He had told me a story about a man who had stumbled upon a nest of impundulu hatchlings. The impundulu, like most animals, were protective of their young and fought to keep them safe. Once they marked you as a threat, they would hunt you down even after you left their territory. It was silly to leave the nest unprotected, but who's going to tell that to a sixty-pound angry bird?

The impundulu hunted the man and caught him three times. The first time the bird plucked out one of the man's eyes, but he got away. The second time the man shot an arrow through one of the bird's wings and escaped again. The third time the man lay on the ground pretending to already be dead, to ambush the bird. When the impundulu got close, it could smell that the man was very much alive. It impaled him with the spines on its underbelly before the man could strike.

Most of my father's stories were goofy and funny and fantastical. This one was sad. In the end, the impundulu carried the man back to its nest to, *well*, feed its hatchlings. Papa said that the man didn't know that impundulu had bad peripheral eyesight. That meant not seeing well out of the corner of your eyes. If the man had learned from the first two attacks, he might've survived.

When Frankie's hands glowed with the beginning of her force field, I snapped out of my memories. We needed her magic now.

"I don't like the way they're looking at us," Eli said, his voice shaking.

"They have poor peripheral vision." I shifted into a

defensive position with my legs wider. "As long as we stay out of their direct line of sight, we can confuse them and run away."

Scratch that: two more impundulu landed in the cornfield. They had us surrounded. So much for their vision problem. No matter which way we moved, we would be in one of the birds' lines of sight. They were smart, and before we had a chance to think of another plan, they screeched all at once. Sharp pain tore through my body, and I fell to my knees. Frankie and Eli fell too, covering their ears. All four birds wasted no time coming for us, and we had nowhere to run.

Sixteen

When I almost become bird food

THE IMPUNDULU SPREAD their rainbow wings and shrieked again. The air rippled around them as white light flashed behind my eyes. Sharp pain sliced through my skull. We covered our ears to block out their cries, but that only helped a little. Frankie got off a blast of energy that narrowly missed hitting one of the birds. That stopped them from advancing on us.

The bird cocked its head to the side to look at the impundulu to its right. Its shrieks stretched into long notes that sounded like nails on a chalkboard. Its fellow giant killer bird answered in the same pitch. It was an *answer*. No mistaking the way they exchanged glances. They were figuring out how best to attack. It didn't escape my attention that these impundulu still had blood on their spines from their last kill.

"Ahhh," Eli shouted as we climbed to our feet. "We have to stop them from screaming."

The killer birds surrounded us as we stood back-to-back. I stared down helplessly at the staff on the ground, but I couldn't get it without uncovering my ears. Our only break from the noise was when the impundulu sucked in more air for their next terrible cry.

I swallowed the knot in my throat—an idea brewing in my head. "We have to make them run into each other."

Eli forced a laugh. "Talk about running around like a chicken with his head cut off."

"You do realize that you have the worst timing for jokes," said Frankie.

I didn't mind so much. I needed the distraction. That way I could stop thinking about the impundulu tearing us to shreds.

We froze when the impundulu stopped shrieking. That is, stopped planning how they were going to eat us. Before we could make a move, the birds tucked their heads between their hunched shoulders and charged. They ran straight for us, their wings fluttering wildly and their bloody spines fanned out for maxium damage. I thought we were goners for sure.

We made ourselves stand still, hearts pounding. As the

impundulu got closer, it wasn't fear that kept us rooted in place. It was strategy. The four birds were closing in fast, and if we got the timing right, they would crash into each other.

One, two, three, I counted in my head. "Now!"

We dove out of the way, and only two of the impundulu collided. It wasn't pretty. My stomach lurched seeing the birds tangled up like that. Each impaled on the other's spines. There was so much blood, and I couldn't catch my breath as I snatched up the staff. The other impundulu skidded to a halt.

The two tangled birds fell into a heap of twisted spines and feathers and blood while the other two took to the sky. Their bright wings spanned twenty feet and blocked the little light to be had from the blue moon. We ran through the high grass along the edge of the cornfield away from the angry birds. I stumbled more times than I could count, but we kept going, afraid to look over our shoulders.

If there was one word I would use to describe the impundulu, it would be *single-minded*. They didn't stop to mourn their fallen comrades. If anything, they redoubled their effort to kill us. I ducked right when one swooped down at me. Not fast enough. Its talons raked across my shoulder, and I bit back a scream as searing pain brought me to my knees. The bird shrieked, coming at me again, and I rolled out of the way. I fell on my back and slammed the staff into the impundulu's side. The impact sent the bird tumbling into a cornstalk.

I winced at the pain in my shoulder and struggled to my feet. The other impundulu clawed Frankie across her pant leg, and Eli threw a rock that hit the bird in the gut. The impundulu whirled around, face screwed up in an unmistakable look of indignation. Eli had the prods out. This time, he was ready for it.

The bird charged, and Eli backed away, stumbled, and almost fell. Frankie sent a ripple of energy that hit the impundulu and sent it hurtling through the air. It slammed into a tree and knocked itself out cold. Here was a new thing I learned about the impundulu: they weren't *that* smart. The bird that I hit with Papa's staff was on its feet again. You'd think after seeing us take down three of its friends, the impundulu would count its losses and run, but it didn't. Maybe it wanted revenge. It looked at each of us, sizing up which one to take on.

The impundulu gave one last battle cry, then headed straight for Eli. I raced between it and my friend with my staff ready, then whacked the bird across the back of its head. The impundulu collapsed to the ground. Neither it nor the one that Frankie hit looked dead, but they most certainly were unconscious.

We stood in the field trying to catch our breath. In the little time we'd been in the Dark, the sky had deepened to midnight blue. If I thought *the Dark* was a misnomer, that the name didn't mean anything, I was dead wrong. It was much darker than the nights back home without streetlights.

"We should be in the exact location of the convention center in our world," I said, looking around. "If that's how a parallel dimension actually works."

"Yes." Frankie straightened her glasses. "Except this area hasn't been developed yet in the Dark. And it looks like the Midwest here is also known for cornfields."

Eli picked at one of the stalks. "This corn is black."

"We have black corn back home," Frankie said, unimpressed.

Eli peeled back the husk on the corn, and light pulsed around the kernels. "We don't have *glowing* black corn."

"Fascinating!" Frankie leaned in to get a closer look. "I wonder if—"

"Wonder later," I said, pulling out my compass. We couldn't let ourselves be so easily distracted; we had to find my father. "I've been thinking about this epicenter thing again. Especially the part about where it all started for me . . . I think the Lord of Shadows means when I first saw the world turn gray at . . ."

"At school?" Eli frowned.

I nodded—even if I knew it didn't make sense. "In Ms. Vanderbilt's class."

Eli stuffed the prods into his backpack. "I thought your father was supposed to be *here*."

"I'm not following, Maya," added Frankie.

I flipped open the compass, wincing at the pain in my shoulder. "I think the Lord of Shadows took my father to the location where Jackson Middle would be in the Dark." That was the best clue I had, and now that I said it out loud, it didn't sound that convincing. "The geographical location, I mean."

"If I understood the cranky twins' explanation of how the veil works, there's only one earth." Frankie's eyebrows pinched together. "The tectonic shifts that made seven continents in our world should've happened in the Dark too. So the landmass *should* be the same."

"We need to head southeast where Chicago would be," I said, studying the compass.

Eli pointed at my shoulder. "That looks bad."

Frankie pulled off her backpack. "I have a first-aid kit . . . Let's get that patched up first."

The cuts hurt, and I could feel blood gushing out of the wound, but that was the least of my concerns. Three dark-bringers stood on the edge of the cornfield staring in our direction. The first-aid kit would have to wait. In all our running around from the impundulu, we'd made a ruckus. Now with our injuries, we were in no shape for another fight.

The darkbringers were twenty feet away—close enough that I could see that they were no taller than us. From their small horns and the small barbs on their tails, they could have been children too. The one in the middle looked no older than Eli's baby sister, Jayla. They didn't move—probably shocked to see humans in the Dark, or maybe they thought we were aliens from outer space.

"Later," I whispered as Frankie unzipped her backpack.

These darkbringers didn't change their shape, and they didn't attack. I had a bad feeling about this. That feeling only grew worse when the one in the middle stepped forward and screamed. It was a petulant little kid's scream, but it finally got Frankie's attention. Her head snapped up from digging around in her backpack for the first-aid kit. All of a sudden, vines covered in thorns shot up from the ground and whipped around Frankie's feet. She cried out as she hit the dirt.

More vines were sprouting up everywhere, thrashing and wriggling toward us. Eli sprang to action. He used his shirttail to cover his hands as he clawed at the vines around Frankie's ankles.

"Stop hurting my friends!" I slammed the staff into the ground, giving it the order to burn the vines.

A spark leaped from the staff. At first, I thought the magic had failed, but then fire flared to life on top of a vine writhing toward me.

Hope lit inside me too as the fire spread to vine after vine. It consumed the ones latched on to Frankie's legs, but the flames skipped across her skin. It understood that she was my friend and wouldn't hurt her.

Eli helped Frankie to her feet as we watched the fire grow bigger and spread. Sweat beaded on my forehead, and I swiped it away. My friends were sweating too. The longer the fire burned, the more speed it picked up. I shifted on my heels, my heart racing against my chest. Before long, the fire had grown into a full raging inferno that burned across the cornfield. To my horror, it headed straight for the dark-bringers and the little one in the middle, who started to cry.

SEVENTEEN

THERE'S NOWHERE TO HIDE IN THE DARK

I WAS HELPLESS as the fire burned through the cornfield. I had only meant to free my friend, and now I'd lost control of the staff. "Please stop," I said under my breath. "Please." But no amount of begging worked, and if anything, the flames burned brighter. The smoke filling the air burned my eyes as the two impundulu we'd knocked unconscious woke with a start. Soon they flapped their wings and flew away. It was bad enough that we'd destroyed their nest and tricked the other two into running into each other. I never wanted to cause so much death and destruction. I only wanted to find Papa and go home.

Now the fire raced toward the three darkbringers at the edge of the field. *Toward the kids*. With the light from the flames, I could see for sure that the two darkbringers on the ends were around our age. The one in the middle was even younger. I could make out a little gray barn and, farther away, a house behind them.

All three had ram horns that curved across their dark hair. Although they stared at the fire with wide eyes, none moved a muscle, except for the little girl in the middle. She buried her face against the boy's leg. He wrapped an arm around her and pulled her closer. The same way Eli had protected Jayla when the darkbringers attacked our neighborhood. We were the invaders now, and it made me question everything I knew about the Dark and the darkbringers. Which, admittedly, wasn't very much.

"Why aren't you running away?" I screamed. "*Go!*"

Eli stiffened at my side, and I wondered if the little darkbringer girl reminded him of his sister too. "Stop the fire, Maya," he pleaded. "You've made your point."

I clutched the staff, again begging it to put the flames out. I begged for rain. When my commands failed, I told the staff to spare the darkbringer children. It didn't listen. The fire would reach them any minute now.

Sweat trickled down my back. "I can't control it."

"You have to control it!" Eli yelled. "Those are kids."

I hadn't come to the Dark to fight anyone. I just wanted to free my father. I hadn't thought through the consequences of our actions either. Sure, I knew that our parents would ground us for sneaking out. But that was minor compared to the *real* consequences. That I might have to hurt many people to get Papa back. My pulse rang in my ears, and my hands trembled. This was different from fighting the darkbringers who tried to kill us at Comic-Con. These darkbringers just stood there like they had a death wish.

I'd always known that we wouldn't walk into the Dark and find Papa without a fight. But at the same time, I never doubted that I could get him back. Oshun, the orisha of beauty, had warned me about my vanity. She'd said, *You don't know enough to know what you don't know.* And she was right. I didn't even know how to control Papa's staff. Not fully. How could I be the future guardian of the veil when I couldn't get this right?

"Run!" I shouted again, waving my arms at the darkbringers. "Get out of the way!"

Eli and Frankie did the same. The two older kids looked at each other and said something too low for us to hear, but they didn't move.

A thousand thoughts raced through my mind. How could I stop the fire from reaching the other kids? How could we save my father without fighting every single time we met a darkbringer?

When the wall of fire almost reached them, the boy's eyes began to glow white. The fire stopped cold. It didn't go out; it simply froze like he had put a barrier around it.

"I don't know if we should be relieved or worried," Eli said under his breath.

The older girl picked up a rock and threw it at us. The rock spun through the air, and as it did, more rocks lifted from the ground and joined it. At first only a dozen, then more and more. The rocks started to multiply themselves the closer they got. One rock we could dodge, but a hundred, no way. Not in an open field with no place to hide.

"I'm going with . . . *worried*," Frankie chimed in.

We ran, but the rocks kept coming and picking up speed. They corrected their courses to keep pace with us. I spotted a point where the field sloped downhill out of sight of the darkbringers—and got an idea.

"Down there!" I said, taking a sharp turn toward the slope.

We ran full speed ahead, using our last energy to barrel downhill. Unfortunately, we miscalculated our velocity. Eli bumped into me, and I bumped into Frankie. We didn't so much as run down the hill as, um, *roll*. We landed at the bottom with a hard thud in a bed of soft moss that broke our fall. The rocks soared over our heads, then fell all at once. I suspected the girl controlling them had given up now that we were out of her sight.

I climbed to my feet, half out of breath, and scooped up the staff. "That was a close call."

Eli brushed dirt off his jeans. "Running for your life totally sucks."

I scanned our surroundings, looking for a place we could hide so we could rest. It was going to be a long night. My eyes landed on a cluster of towering lights in the distance, and my heart leaped in my chest. I pulled out the compass to check the direction. The city was due southeast, where Chicago would be. At least that wasn't different in the Dark, but the city's skyline was wrong. It was most definitely *not* our Chicago.

"The epicenter of where it all began," Frankie said from behind me, her voice pained.

I nodded, knowing that the Lord of Shadows would not make this easy.

Eli adjusted his backpack. "I'm not one to complain *much,* but we need a break. We're in no shape to walk that far. It'll take hours."

"I don't think I can actually walk," Frankie added.

Eli and I whirled around to see Frankie on the ground cradling her leg. "I think those vines were poisonous."

I winced as I knelt beside her. Pushing back my own

pain, I helped Frankie roll up her pants. Her leg was swollen and covered in black veins.

If I ever wished the cranky Johnston twins were around, it was now. Miss Lucille had healed our injuries after the darkbringers attacked at the park and we needed her help. The black veins were worse where the thorns had cut Frankie's ankle. Some stretched up to her knee. This was my fault for bringing my friends here. I had to do something before the infection got worse.

"I can try to use the staff . . . see if it helps," I suggested.

"You can't even control that thing!" Eli yelled. "What if you make it worse?"

I ducked my head, feeling awful about everything.

"Try the staff," Frankie said, ignoring Eli. "I trust you."

"I trust her too!" Eli shrugged. "It's the staff I don't trust."

Frankie glanced over her shoulder. "I'd feel better if we put some distance between us and them first."

I spotted a line of trees in the opposite direction from where we needed to go. Away from Papa, not toward him. I bit my lip, rocking on my heels. "Let's see if we can find a place to camp for the night over there."

Eli and I took turns helping Frankie as we crossed the mossy hills. Of all the things we brought with us, no one had remembered to pack a flashlight. After a while, our eyes began to adjust to the dark. We saw white particles everywhere, in the air, covering the ground, and on us. They were so small and paper-thin that we couldn't really feel them. They looked like a cross between ash and snow and seemed harmless enough. Frankie wanted to stop, but Eli convinced her that now was not the time. She could gather some of the particles to study later.

The darkbringer children had either lost our trail or hadn't bothered to come after us. I hoped that it was the latter, and that they didn't tell their parents, which wasn't likely. Anyone with any sense would tell someone if they saw *weird* people wielding magic. In this case, we were the outsiders. We were the invaders, the aliens. I didn't feel bad about that. They came to our world first and helped the Lord of Shadows kidnap my father. I didn't feel good about it either.

When we reached the forest, I whispered to the staff, "Show us a safe place to rest."

I bit my lip, wondering if it would go haywire again. By some stroke of luck, it didn't. Instead, it pointed to a cave hidden behind two red trees. When I say red, I mean the trunk, bark, and leaves were all red, but we were too tired to gawk at them.

We set up our sleeping bags inside the cave. The ground was a little damp and cold, but it could've been worse. With the staff, I made two rocks glow to give us light to see but not enough to attract attention.

"I hope this works," I said, leaning over Frankie. She had passed out on her sleeping bag the moment we got her into the cave. I inhaled a deep breath to calm my nerves, which helped a little. I tapped Frankie's ankle and whispered to the staff again. The symbols lit up and rearranged themselves, then the light filled the entire cave. Sparks of light separated out into little fireflies that landed on Eli and me too. Then the light went away. Frankie still had her injury. I tried again, but the staff didn't respond.

"Told you." Eli sat with his knees tucked against his chest. "Can't trust it."

I let out a frustrated sigh and bit my tongue. I didn't need him rubbing it in my face. "We'll get Frankie back to the gateway first thing in the morning if she's not better."

"Let me put a ping on our location so we have a reference point back to the gateway. I should have thought of this before the killer birds showed up." Eli pulled out his phone. He slid his finger across the screen and tapped, his face screwed up into a frown. "I don't have any service."

I sank into my sleeping bag and clutched it around my neck. We'd crossed into another world, and maybe cell towers and cellphones weren't a thing here. With all the magic the darkbringers possessed, they didn't need such *toys*. But I wasn't in the mood to say any of this to Eli.

The smart thing to do would've been to pack up our things and circle back around until we found the gateway to Comic-Con. Go back to the safety of the human world. The veil hadn't failed yet, and I didn't think the dark-bringers would figure out how to use the ancient gateway so soon. But I wasn't going to do the smart thing. I had no intention of running away. In the morning, I would see if Frankie and Eli wanted to go back, but I would stay and find Papa, even if I had to do it on my own.

Eighteen

Three against an army

I **WAS DEAD TIRED** when I balled up in my sleeping bag. Everything hurt: my back, my shoulder, my legs, and my feet. I couldn't sleep while listening to Frankie's choppy, uneven breathing. I could never forgive myself if she . . . No, I couldn't even think it. She was going to be okay.

"Mommy's gone?" she mumbled in her sleep.

I shivered at the pain in her voice. She'd once told me about her first mom—how one day she'd gone to the store for groceries and never returned. The police said that her mom had died in a car accident. Now that I thought about it, that didn't add up, especially since she was an orisha. She was immortal—no accident could've killed her. I would never pry or ask more questions, but I wondered what really happened to her.

When I finally fell asleep, I dreamt that the Lord of Shadows crawled into the cave and stole Frankie away. His ribbons wrapped her up like a mummy, and as they did, her face and hair turned gray. When I ran after her, I caught up with them in Ms. Vanderbilt's class. The Lord of Shadows was sitting at my math teacher's desk, grading papers, his ribbons climbing up the walls. Frankie was at the chalkboard writing:

THE PLACE IT ALL BEGAN FOR YOU.
THE PLACE IT ALL BEGAN FOR YOU.
THE PLACE IT ALL BEGAN FOR YOU.

The dream startled me awake at daybreak, and the absurdity of it hit me at once. The only thing that made me feel better was that it had been an *actual* dream, not another visit from the Lord of Shadows. It was a reminder that I couldn't stay here hiding in a cave. I needed to get to the place in the Dark where Jackson Middle should be, and deep down I knew that I was running out of time.

The morning was only a few shades lighter than the night. Everything looked bruised purple, like the sky before a storm. Eli and I packed up our things and left Frankie sleeping for a while longer. She was finally resting without tossing and turning, and we didn't want to disturb her. I left Papa's staff against the cave wall and paced back and forth. The red forest was even more frightening during the day. Sap that looked and smelled like blood seeped from the bark. When the wind rustled the leaves, they made a weeping sound. With a bit more light, the ash particles we saw last night were flecks of dust out of the corner of our eyes. I couldn't help but wonder if they were alive. The way they floated in the air seemed coordinated.

Eli frowned at me as he removed an apple and a bottle of water from his bag. "All my injuries are gone, but why isn't Frankie better?"

I stopped in my tracks, feeling like a failure. "I don't know . . . My injuries healed too."

"What if she . . ." he said, but his voice cut off.

"I'm not going to die," Frankie said from behind me. She stood in the mouth of the cave looking a little gray.

"You're better!" I said. Her leg still looked awful, but some of the black veins had disappeared and it was less swollen.

She stumbled forward. "Almost as good as new."

Eli rushed to help her and ducked his head when she thanked him.

We settled down to eat, and Frankie drank a whole bottle of water. "You two should go back," I said. "What happened last night . . . it could've been worse."

Frankie pinched her chapped lips. "We're in this together."

Eli bit into his apple and said, "We can't go back to hide, and it won't matter anyway if the veil fails."

"I . . . I just . . ." I stuttered.

Frankie grimaced, and I didn't finish my sentence.

I just don't want anything to happen to you, I wanted to say. Instead I pulled out the compass. "We keep moving." I stared down so I wouldn't meet my friends' eyes. I was glad they would stay with me but felt bad too. "I mapped the trip before we left. It should take about seven hours to get to where Jackson Middle School would be in Chicago."

"After last night," Eli said, "we need to do a better job of keeping out of sight."

After breakfast we broke camp and set off. It took some practice to navigate with the compass, especially through the forest. Once we were out, we ran into more farmlands. We did a lot of circling back to avoid them and hiding when we heard a sound.

"This is going to take longer than seven hours," Frankie said, once we cleared a stretch of farmlands. Her leg had healed completely, and she looked almost back to normal.

Now we were walking on the shoulder of a gravel road—and I wondered what type of transportation the darkbringers had here. We hadn't seen any vehicles since we started our trek.

"I may have miscalculated," I said, embarrassed. "I didn't

think about all the time we would waste hiding from the darkbringers."

Eli pointed toward the city. "But we *are* getting closer."

He was right. If we kept going, we could be there by nightfall. From here the city appeared to be a perfect circle with a ring of shorter buildings around the edge. Each inner ring of buildings was a little taller than the ones before it. This went on until the buildings in the middle of the circle were the tallest of them all. I squeezed the staff and pushed down my fears. No way we'd be able to avoid every single darkbringer, so maybe night was our best chance. But I remembered what Papa said: *The enemy is strongest under the cover of darkness.* It was yet another risk we had to take.

I saw something coming our way fast. It was some sort of helicopter that had left the city. The shape of the craft was weird, and it flew too close to the ground. As it drew closer, an annoying buzzing sound filled the air.

"Hide!" I shouted, and we ducked into the tall, neon-green weeds beside the road. Not the best cover by a long shot, but it was all we had. We couldn't get caught now, not when we were only a few hours from the epicenter.

The sound grew louder, and I gritted my teeth, ready to use the staff, but I hoped I wouldn't have to.

"Don't see us," Eli whispered, his voice desperate as the craft flew over our position. "Keep going."

Bugacopter was the perfect name for the thing. It looked like an overgrown fly. It had two gigantic eyes, metal wings, and a glass dome where the body would be if it were a real insect. The annoying buzzing sound was coming from its wings. And the worst part was the darkbringer in the glass dome at the controls had his eyes pinned on us.

I guessed a day without fighting was too much to hope for. The bugacopter stopped above us — its wings kicking up grass and dirt that stung my eyes. Frankie was still too weak to call her energy. It was Eli who reacted first. He whipped out the prods he took from the darkbringer at Comic-Con and slammed them into the glass dome. An electrical current flickered down the length of the prods, then shot through the craft. Long cracks spread across the glass.

"Watch out!" I shouted as the craft wobbled.

The pilot yanked at the controls as the wings flapped wildly. He pulled up but didn't get very far before the craft crashed a few feet away.

We gasped in horror as the craft burst into flames. Eli stuffed the prods back in his backpack with shaking hands. It was either the darkbringer or us. Knowing that we had no choice didn't make the knot in my stomach go away.

"We have to go." Frankie nudged Eli's arm, and he snapped out of his trance.

We hurried toward the city again, staying as far away

from the road as we could. After the accident, none of us was in the mood to talk. I couldn't get the image of the helicopter crashing and bursting into flames out of my head. Eli slipped into a blank stare, and Frankie did too.

We had only walked another hour when we almost ran straight into three darkbringers near a farm. Before they could spot us, we ducked behind an old shed. From the looks of them, they'd just finished searching the grounds. Unlike the darkbringers who'd attacked us back home, these darkbringers spoke in a language that was efficient and clipped with sharp edges. I hadn't thought about it before, but some of them had to know a lot about the human world while we knew nothing about their world.

I squeezed the staff and wished that we knew what they were saying. The symbols on the staff pulsed, and I could feel my ears and tongue tingling like when I ate Pop Rocks. Suddenly we could understand the darkbringers' language, and the news was *not* good.

"We've quarantined this sector, sir," came a gruff voice. "They will not escape."

The darkbringers hurried north, and we dodged them on our way south. Every few minutes we had to drop to our bellies to hide in the tall grass to avoid being caught. They were everywhere. In avoiding one group, we ran straight into two burly darkbringers. The men startled when they saw us. Instead of attacking, they gawked like we were some exotic species. We stared at them too.

One of the darkbringers raised a shell to his lips and blew. It echoed across the field, as loud as a bullhorn, and turned my blood cold. He was calling for backup, and that realization snapped me and my friends out of our daze. Frankie and I both sent a powerful force that knocked the darkbringers on their butts. We ran, our legs pumping hard, but there was nowhere to go. Darkbringers were coming from every direction.

This was the exact thing we'd been trying to avoid. Another confrontation. It was too late for that now as dozens of darkbringers stomped through the high grass, hot on our trail. Out of options, we stopped to catch our breath before the impending fight. I shifted so the staff crisscrossed my body, ready to strike the first darkbringer who got too close. I wouldn't let them stand in my way of finding Papa.

"I need a distraction," Eli said, his hands balled into fists.

"I don't think a distraction is going to help us right now," I said as the darkbringers closed in. "We have to fight."

Eli bit his lip in concentration. "Maya, please, just do it!"

Frankie and I glanced at each other. I thought that Eli was finally about to lose it, but there was a look of pure determination in his eyes. I raised the staff over my head and asked it to call a storm. As soon as the first lightning bolt struck the ground, the darkbringers paused. Some turned to look at the sudden dark clouds rolling across the already dusky sky.

"What are you doing?" I asked.

"Shush," Eli said as his skin began to shimmer.

Frankie gaped and stumbled back a step. "Is he . . ."

Before she could finish speaking, Eli turned semi-transparent. We could see him and see through him. Then he completely . . . *disappeared.*

"*Ummm,* Eli?" I whispered.

He replied with a low snicker, then I felt a tap on my shoulder. A blue shimmering light settled over me and Frankie too, and we began to become transparent. We were able to see Eli again — he looked like a ghost out of a horror flick with that twisted grin on his face.

"Where did they go?" one of the darkbringers snarled.

When another one ran straight past us, oblivious to our new state, Eli whispered, "Told you so."

It figured that a boy obsessed with everything paranormal could turn us invisible. Eli had discovered his godling power.

NINETEEN

We meet our match

HAD WE STILL BEEN at Comic-Con, these dark-bringers would've fit right in as the latest super soldiers built in Dr. Z's lab. They looked like thick-necked wrestlers without the spandex or the cool catch phrases. They wore black uniforms, vests laden with knives, and battleaxes across their backs. Too bad we didn't have Oya to put an end to them.

Eli's magic held as we quietly continued our trek toward the city. It shimmered across our skin, making us invisible to the darkbringers. They stalked around the field with their eyes narrowed and their weapons in their hands. My friends and I could see each other, except we were semitransparent. It might not have been the ghost army that Eli wanted, but I was grateful that his magic finally showed. It gave me hope that my magic would come someday too.

"The commander is on the way," whispered one dark-bringer to another.

It was a boy not much older than us talking to a girl who looked around the same age. "Oh no, she's in a bad mood," said the girl looking to the sky.

"How do you know?" asked the boy, sounding like he had a lump in his throat.

The girl leaned closer to him and said, "Her wings are only that color when she's mad."

"Oh." He looked as scared as I felt when I saw the commander flying toward our position.

I couldn't figure out where her wings began or where they ended. They spanned the sky, like a colorful hang glider mounted against her back. A rainbow of colors danced across them as she dipped and adjusted her flight path. If a butterfly's wings were beautiful, then hers were a word I'd never used but had heard: *exquisite*.

"She sawed off the last rookie's horns for giving her the stink eye," the girl said.

Eli and Frankie winced beside me. I winced too. We'd gone from bad to worse *again*. I was beginning to think the universe was playing a dirty trick on us. Two dozen darkbringers stopped searching for us in the field to wait for the commander to land. We couldn't risk someone hearing our footsteps in the dry grass, so we had to stop too.

As much as my knees shook, I couldn't help but be a little amazed. The commander moved like she owned the sky, and even a flock of birds got out of her way. Before I could release the breath pinned in my chest, she landed on the ground. She wasn't blue and didn't have horns either. She was brown, not dark like me or Frankie, or light like Eli. She was golden.

It took me a minute to figure out that she was from the aziza people Papa mentioned in one of his stories. The aziza were faeries notorious for not interacting with outsiders. I hadn't expected to see one running a darkbringer army. I hadn't expected a lot of things that seemed commonplace in the Dark. Papa had said that the aziza were so lovely they enchanted you with their songbird language. One had enchanted him once, but he didn't tell that story.

This aziza spoke the darkbringers' language, and her voice was musical.

"Report," she demanded, looking at no one in particular. I wondered how she'd come to be in the Dark. "Where are they?"

The two dozen darkbringers stood stiff. They all looked like they could crack stone with their teeth or cut you in two with their barbed tails. But they also looked scared of this aziza, who had a face that said *mess with me and die a slow, painful death.*

"Commander Nulan, sir." One of the older dark-bringers with bright blue skin fell in step beside her. Nulan had folded her wings against her back and now strolled through the ranks of soldiers. "No sign of them yet, but we have the valley completely barricaded, and we're bringing in hounds."

The commander wrinkled her nose. "You need hounds to do your job for you, is that it?"

"No, sir." The older darkbringer answered too fast to be as calm as he pretended. "We aren't trackers; we're foot soldiers, first on the line," he explained. "With that said, we've picked up their scent, but the wind has spread it across the valley."

"I don't want excuses," Nulan barked. "Our lord felt them enter our world, and he wants them found now. They couldn't have gone far."

The words *our lord* rang in my ears, and my heart leaped against my chest. The Lord of Shadows knew that I would come. He'd dared me to, so that was no surprise. Still, it made me realize that no matter what, eventually I would have to face him. Not on the crossroads—*in the flesh.* He wouldn't hesitate to kill me and my friends like he'd done to Papa's previous family. I didn't know how I could defeat an enemy so powerful, but I knew I had to be ready for anything.

"Find them!" Nulan said through gritted teeth.

Frankie twitched next to me at the fire in Nulan's voice. I didn't like this woman one bit, and she was standing between us and the city where my father was being held captive. At her command, the darkbringers started searching the field again. We had to escape, while Eli's invisibility magic still held.

I tapped my friends on their shoulders and pointed out a path through the darkbringers. Frankie and Eli nodded back to let me know that they understood the plan. We fell into a single line with Frankie in front, Eli in the middle, and me bringing up the rear. We only needed the magic to hold a little longer, until we cleared the field and left the darkbringers behind. I clutched the staff hard as we took one careful step after another. The city was so close now. Only an hour or two away at the most. *I'm coming, Papa.*

Even though the field was huge, we had to zigzag a lot to avoid the darkbringers. One would've barreled right into Frankie if Eli hadn't pushed her out of the way. Another one was sweeping his long tail in the air and almost struck my arm. This was *not* easy, and it was slow.

"We found evidence that they were sleeping in a cave in

a forest," the older darkbringer reported to the commander. "We found these little black seeds."

Black seeds? I tried to think of what they were and remembered that Eli had eaten an apple. He shrugged as we crept further away, almost clear of the darkbringers. *Almost.*

"I don't care about where they were sleeping," Nulan shouted. "I want them, and I want them now!"

"Are you sure those are not their droppings?" Another darkbringer laughed.

And I thought Eli had bad timing with his jokes. This guy was worse.

We had made it through the last of the darkbringers when Frankie stepped on a twig, and it snapped. Several darkbringers spun around, and we froze.

"Halt!" Nulan yelled.

Frankie winced, and Eli mouthed a curse that would've gotten him grounded for a month had Nana been here.

Nulan elbowed her way to where the darkbringers stared in our direction. "What is it?"

"A sound from over there, sir," one of them answered.

Nulan smiled. It was an ugly, twisted smile that destroyed any pretense of beauty. "So, it seems the intruders are right under our noses."

We stood there shaking, me with Papa's staff shimmering with magic. Frankie with her palms facing out, ready to send a blast of power. Eli with his invisibility cloak still in place.

The commander turned her back and whispered something to the older darkbringer. He made a gesture, and the other darkbringers moved until they had surrounded us.

Without warning, Nulan whirled around and blew on her hand. Flecks of gold and silver spread across the valley. To our horror, they landed on us too, and the commander smiled again.

"There you are," she said.

The darkbringers pulled their weapons. Eli grumbled and released his invisibility magic. It was time to fight.

The darkbringers stared at us with wide eyes. Even Commander Nulan looked surprised. Frankie, Eli, and I had felt the same when we saw the darkbringers in the park in our neighborhood. This was probably the first time that some of them had seen humans, or well, godlings.

It made no sense that they wanted to wage war on people they didn't know or understand. Yes, humans and darkbringers looked different, but that didn't matter. Didn't they see that the Lord of Shadows only wanted revenge?

"We're not here to make trouble." I forced my voice to sound strong, but I didn't think they were buying my act. "We're sorry about the cornfield. That was an accident."

"The other darkbringers attacked us first." Eli frowned. "At least I think they did." He didn't look so sure, and I wasn't convinced anymore either. The fire had gone after them *before* the girl sent rocks hurtling at us.

"What he means is that," Frankie added, "this is all a big misunderstanding."

Anyone with half a brain could see that we were stalling for time to come up with a plan.

"Elegguá's spawn"—Nulan spat out, ignoring everything we'd said—"and her friends. So pathetic."

"Kill them." One of the darkbringers reared back his ax, and the others followed.

"No, you fools," Nulan hissed. "We'll take them—"

The words were barely out of her mouth when the same darkbringer flung his ax at me. It soared through the air, hissing as it did. Without thinking, I lifted the staff vertically and spun it across my body. The white symbols glowed, turning the ax into ashes, which fell to the ground only a split second from hitting me.

Nulan reached into her black vest and removed a slim knife of her own, her eyes on Papa's staff the whole time. She flipped her wrist so fast that the knife was a silver blur. Eli gasped, and for one horrible moment, I thought he was hurt. Then I saw that Nulan had aimed the blade for the darkbringer who went against her order. He stumbled and fell to his knees with the knife lodged in his chest. She'd killed him—*one of her own men.* I had no doubt that she'd do the same to us if we couldn't get out of this situation, and fast.

"I said that we'll take these little godlings to the Lord of Shadows alive," she said, her voice slippery sweet. "Does anyone else have an objection?"

The darkbringers growled and spat on the ground. Some cursed, glaring at *me* with murder in their eyes. They hated my father, and they hated me too. How could I make them understand that he made a mistake the first time with the veil? That now, this war the Lord of Shadows wanted was wrong? It could only bring about death for both our worlds.

"Good," Nulan said, satisfied when no one answered her.

"We're not going to let you take us," Frankie said, her palms aimed at Nulan.

The commander tilted her head to one side, her face contemplative. "On second thought, I don't need all of you." Nulan removed another slim knife from her vest and sent it flying straight for Frankie's heart. I lifted Papa's staff to counter her attack, but nothing happened. The symbols didn't glow, they didn't move. Nothing.

Frankie sent balls of light at Nulan that dissipated mid-air. One of the darkbringers must've been countering our magic. Just as the knife was inches from my friend, I leaped in front of her. Everything was a blur as I raised the staff to deflect the knife. But before I could, the ground shook hard beneath our feet, then it opened up and swallowed us whole.

TWENTY

WE GET STUCK IN A HOLE

WE FELL THROUGH an endless black hole into a place that couldn't exist without magic. It wasn't underground, but another crossroads, a place between places — *an abyss*. I couldn't see my friends in the dark, but we kept floating into each other like astronauts on a spaceship.

"Well, this is inconvenient," Eli whispered, "and in the middle of a fight too."

We had to whisper here because our voices vibrated the space around us like an earthquake. If we talked too loud, the tremors were ten times worse.

"A fight we were *losing*," Frankie said, sarcasm lacing her words.

I couldn't stop thinking about how things had gone so wrong. How could I be the future guardian of the veil if I couldn't even last a full day in the Dark? We were so close to finding Papa.

I swallowed the bitter taste on my tongue as the memory of the oddly circular city taunted me. Papa was there—only hours away, and we blew it. No, *I* blew it. I knew the Lord of Shadows wouldn't just let me waltz into the Dark to get my father back. I should've been more prepared.

"What am I going to do now?" I mumbled under my breath.

I said it too low for my friends to hear and quietly swiped tears from my cheeks.

I was mad at myself, but I was mad at the orishas too. Why couldn't they help instead of waiting for the other celestials to come first? By now Mama, Frankie's moms, and Nana had to know that we'd found a way into the Dark.

I bit my lip and pushed those thoughts out of my mind. I couldn't stand around—*um, float around*—feeling sorry for myself. I had to figure out how to go back into the Dark —and this time get it right.

"This place is like the metal detector at the community center," I blurted out. "Like the gateway into the Dark too, but somehow different."

"Yeah, but both of those were very fast," Eli said. "We didn't hang out in limbo."

"What happens when a portal has mechanical problems?" I asked.

"Machines have mechanical problems," Eli said, "not giant holes in the ground."

"Maya's right," Frankie chipped in, her voice bright. "It's like we're stuck on an elevator between floors."

"What if we can't get out?" Eli groaned. "Who's going to take Jayla on piggyback rides and play monster hunt with her in the garden?"

"We'll get out." I tried to reassure the both of us. "If there's a way in, then there's a way out, right?"

"How did we even get here?" Eli asked.

"I don't know . . ." I answered, racking my brains. The staff had malfunctioned in the fight against Nulan, but I didn't remember feeling its magic before the ground swallowed us up.

"I think this might be a wormhole," Frankie said, oblivious to our conversation. Even in the dark, I imagined her adjusting her glasses, her nose screwed up in her thinking face. "It could be that we're still moving but at such a slow speed it seems like we're floating. We could be traveling tens of thousands of light years as we speak."

"Plain English, please," Eli said, impatient. I imagined *him* rolling his eyes.

"A light year is the measurement of how far light travels over a year," Frankie said. "Which is about six trillion miles."

"Oh man, does that mean we're going to end up on top

of the Dark's version of Mount Everest in the Himalayas?" Eli asked, stunning both Frankie and me into silence. He couldn't be serious. When neither of us answered, he said, "You know, between China and Tibet."

"We know, Eli." I sighed. "Frankie meant somewhere in a faraway galaxy."

"Let me try something," Frankie said, then shortly after that, sparks of light lit up the darkness around us. Her hands glowed, and she aimed them in front of her into the abyss where her light didn't reach.

We waited, but nothing happened, and her light dimmed with each second that passed. "I don't know why it's not working," she said, frustrated. "I can feel the magic, but it's like the darkness is absorbing it."

Eli made himself invisible. "Welp! I'm still stuck here whether you see me or not."

"I'm going to try the staff," I said, after Eli changed himself back to normal and Frankie's light fizzed out.

I grasped the middle of the staff and held it horizontally against my chest. "Grab on," I said to my friends. It took a minute for them to find the staff in the dark, but eventually they both clamped down on either side of me.

I focused hard on wanting to be out of the black abyss. Sweat rolled down my forehead and my back as the magic tingled up my arm. We began to fall, slowly at first, then so fast that the staff ripped from our hands and we got separated. I screwed my eyes shut, knowing what it would mean when we landed anywhere at this speed. No human could survive it . . . maybe not even godlings.

Right on cue, the dizziness hit. It always showed up at the most inconvenient times, which was *any* time lately. As if the spinning in my head weren't enough, it doubled. It felt like the ground was up and the sky was down, like I was falling and flying at the same time. Then I blacked out.

When I finally opened my eyes, I was lying with one side of my face buried in dirt. There were no darkbringers peering at me with their battleaxes ready. No Commander Nulan with her ugly smile and her sharp knives. That was good at least.

I waited for the dizziness to lessen and lifted my head to look around. Slivers of moonlight poked through towering *green* trees. The moon was its usual milky color instead of blue. I swallowed hard, in disbelief. This couldn't be real. It would mean . . . It would mean that we were back in the human world. We'd left the Dark near nightfall, which would be near sunrise here. If it was night again, then I'd lost a whole day.

"Are you okay?" I groaned as I forced myself to sit up.

I rubbed my forehead as the last of the dizziness faded away.

When my friends didn't answer, I snapped to attention.

I was in a very large forest. Papa's staff was a few feet away, and my backpack hung off a low tree branch, but there was no sign of my friends. My heart started to race. I had to force in deep breaths so my dizziness wouldn't come back.

"Where are you guys?" I called with my hands cupped around my mouth.

I yelled at the top of my lungs, and only the sounds of the night answered me. An owl *hoo hooooo*ed, then came a low grunt in the bushes nearby. My friends couldn't have been far. We'd been side by side during the fall, but the speed had knocked them clear of the staff. What if they were more banged up than me and couldn't reply?

I grabbed the staff and used it to free my backpack. My legs shook as I searched the area around the clearing. I looked behind every bush and tree. No sign of either of them. This was *not* good.

I stopped cold and leaned against a tree, out of breath. I couldn't lose my best friends, too. Ever since Miss Ida told me that Papa was missing, I'd tried to be brave. I didn't back down when things got scary, and I came up with new plans when the old ones failed. My shoulders trembled now, and the night breeze cut through me.

I was alone—*really* alone—and tired. I thought about how Frankie's first mom had gone to buy groceries and never come home. How Eli's parents had left him and his little sister with Nana and hardly ever visited. Tears slipped down my face. It wasn't fair. It was like the universe had put this impossible burden on our backs—on my back.

With tears still running down my face, I pushed myself away from the tree. I knew nothing about velocity, but maybe it was possible that my friends had fallen farther away from me. They could be miles away or, worse, a dimension away. What if the black abyss had spat them back into the Dark?

"Find my friends," I whispered to the staff, and it beamed a light due north. I refused to feel relieved until I saw them with my own two eyes. I started walking again, and my legs wobbled, so I used the staff to bear my weight. I trekked what felt like miles of endless forest. With each step, the ache in my belly grew. I looked for signs: footprints or a piece of cloth tied to a tree branch. If they were okay, then they'd be looking for me too.

As I walked, it was getting darker and colder. I wanted to rest, to sleep, but I couldn't. I had to find my friends first. I only paused to drink from my half-empty bottle of water. The sounds of owls and wolves and lizards scuttling in the brush made me jumpy, but they also were comforting. These sounds were familiar to me, sounds of the human world. After walking for hours, I came upon a hiking trail and a sign. It read DANIEL BOONE NATIONAL FOREST.

I couldn't believe it. I was in Kentucky. I knew it was Kentucky, since Papa and Mama brought me kayaking on the Red River Gorge last summer. So not only was I out of the Dark, but I was in the middle of nowhere and my friends were missing. What else could go wrong?

I wiped sweat from my brow as I looked down one end of the trail, then the other. Even though the temperature had dropped, I still felt overheated like a fire was raging in my belly. The staff wasn't exactly helping; it kept getting confused. One minute it would tell me to go north, then south. One minute it would say go right, and the next, go left; sometimes it walked me in loops.

I was about to head east on another trail when a voice froze me in my tracks.

"There she is!" Eli said. "Finally. I thought it would take all night."

Frankie and Eli stood on the opposite side of the trail, a little ways downhill. I sucked in a deep breath. They were okay.

My friends ran toward me, and we met in the middle. Eli was grinning ear to ear. Frankie wiped her brow, leaving a smudge of dirt across her forehead.

"I was looking everywhere for you," I said, relieved to see them.

"We were looking for you too," Frankie said, her eyes brightening.

"Guess where we are," I moaned, still mad about it. "You're not even going to believe it."

They had matching puzzled looks on their faces.

Eli raised an eyebrow. "Myrtle Beach?"

"Alaska?" Frankie said.

I laughed so hard that I got a cramp in my side. They laughed too. Frankie usually didn't go along with Eli's jokes, but right now, we needed a laugh. My friends were alive and in good spirits after all that we'd been through in the Dark.

When the laughter stopped, I said, "The wormhole brought us back to the human world . . . to *Kentucky* of all places."

"And *you* said that we'd end up light years away on an alien planet." Eli rolled his eyes at Frankie.

Frankie shrugged, laughing again. "Lucky I was wrong then."

"I don't get it." I frowned. I understood enough about how wormholes *theoretically* worked to know that Frankie hadn't been wrong before. "We really could've ended up halfway across the Milky Way, though."

"Relax, Maya!" Frankie slapped my shoulder. "We're allowed to have a little laugh after surviving an elite army by sheer luck."

"An army that will crush us humans like flies if it invades our world," Eli said.

Us humans. This was *not okay.*

"Humans, yes, but what about your ghost army, Eli?" I said to test my theory.

"What about it?" Eli screwed up his nose into a scowl.

For starters, I thought, but didn't say out loud, *you don't have one.*

Instead, I answered, "I thought you said that they could stand against the darkbringers."

"*If* I said that, I was a fool," Eli snapped, all amusement gone from his face.

"*If* he said that." Frankie narrowed her eyes. Was she on to me, like I was on to them? "You knew he was kidding. Ghosts are an unruly bunch to control."

My pulse echoed in my ears. I didn't think about how she'd confirmed that ghosts were in fact real; instead, I shrugged like the whole conversation didn't matter. They bought my act and relaxed too.

One thing I knew for sure. The pair standing in front of me weren't Eli and Frankie by a long shot. They were still missing somewhere in the forest or, worse yet, still trapped in the black abyss or in the Dark.

The *Eli* and *Frankie* standing in front of me were darkbringers.

TWENTY-ONE

I LEARN TO KEEP MY COOL

I WOULD PLAY ALONG with the darkbringers so I could get some information out of them. If I was lucky, I could find out if my father was okay. Did these darkbringers know what happened to my friends too?

"So what do we do next?" I asked. "I don't even know how we got here."

"We're here because someone opened an unstable wormhole," the fake Frankie said. She glared at me like it was my fault, but was it?

The orisha council said the darkbringers couldn't pierce the veil. They could only slip into our world through tears. Papa traveled between the two worlds by creating wormholes. Hope swelled in my chest. I *could* have created the wormhole with his staff by accident.

Frankie glanced up at the night sky. "We need to get back."

"Back to Chicago or back to the Dark?" I asked.

"Back to the Dark," she replied. "Don't you want to save *Elegguá?*"

Heat rushed to my belly at the way she spat my father's name. There was a deep, seething hatred in this darkbringer's voice. She tried to cover it with a thin smile, but it didn't reach her cold, dark eyes.

"Is there anything left to save?" I asked, a lump in my throat. It took everything in me not to burst into tears, but I had to know.

Frankie and Eli gave each other a look before Eli said, "I'm sure he's okay for now."

"Think about it," Frankie added. "If I were the Lord of Shadows, I would want to destroy the Elegguá bloodline so there wouldn't be anyone left to keep the veil standing. I bet he'll want to use your father as bait to get to you first."

"We . . . umm . . . just have to be smarter than him," Eli said, unconvincingly.

I sucked in a deep breath through my teeth. Even if I didn't know whether I could trust what they said, their words still gave me hope that Papa was okay. "How are we going to get back into the Dark?"

"Maybe there's a tear nearby," Frankie said, craning her

neck to peer over my shoulder. Her eyes were eager and greedy, like those of a mouse that's spotted cheese.

Eli stood next to me, waiting to see if I would follow Frankie as she set off. I flashed him a smile with the staff tucked close to my side. "I'll take up the rear," I volunteered, and he grudgingly walked two steps ahead of me beside Frankie.

"I hope we don't cross a rattlesnake's path," I said. "That would be bad."

Eli smirked. "Why would we be afraid of a snake?"

"Because if a rattlesnake bites you, it turns your insides to mush," I said.

While that wasn't exactly true, it was close enough. I needed to keep the darkbringers talking while I came up with a plan. "There are a lot of snakes in the forest. They hide beneath bushes and come out at night to hunt."

"That's nothing," Eli said, but he kept watching where he stepped in case. "Snakes are easy to kill."

"I guess you're right." I shrugged. "A grootslang is definitely worse."

"What would you know about a grootslang?" Eli rolled his eyes at me as we continued to trek through the forest.

Papa had in fact told me stories about the grootslang, which looked like a cross between an elephant and a snake. It had leathery black skin and ivory tusks that were venomous. He said that one had attacked a wildlife reserve when he was in the middle of a work assignment in Ghana. Now I could guess that the grootslang had come through a tear in the veil.

"Only that they're not winning any beauty contests anytime soon," I answered.

The fake Eli frowned in confusion. Maybe they didn't have beauty contests in the Dark, which wasn't exactly a bad thing.

As we hopped over a tree root on the path, I cleared my throat. "Rattlesnakes eat their weight in food every night. I don't know if it's possible for a grootslang to do the same since they're so big."

I could feel the tear that the fake Frankie had been silently leading us to. It crackled in the air, like static that tingled against my skin. I didn't have powers of my own, but it seemed that I had inherited the ability to sense the tear from my father. Even Frankie had to stop several times to catch the tear's trail again. I could only guess that the original tear they came through (if it wasn't the wormhole with my friends and me) had closed and she was hunting out a new one.

"Do you think a bloodhound could beat a cougar?" I asked no one in particular.

"Will you shut up!" Frankie snapped. "We're never going to find the tear if you keep distracting me."

Good. I wanted to keep her distracted until I was ready to make my move. Once I was sure I couldn't get more information out of them, I'd knock them out and go look for my friends.

The staff tingled against my sweaty palm as we finally reached the tear in the veil. A crooked black scar darker than night stretched in front of us in thin air. It looked like the black lightning, which I now knew was the first sign of a fissure forming.

I touched the edge of the tear, and a shock of warmth shot up my arm. The staff lit up.

Eli slapped my hand away, and it took everything inside me to keep from whirling a blow across his head. "You're making it worse," he said, glaring at me. "Don't touch it."

"Or what?" I said, almost losing my temper.

Eli stepped in my face, his hands balled into fists. "Do it again, and you'll see."

Frankie stepped between us and cut her eyes at Eli. An understanding passed between the two darkbringers. "Both of you, stop acting childish," she said. "We have a way back into the Dark, time to go."

I wouldn't let my racing heart stop me from doing the right thing, which was find my friends first. "I'm not going back with you," I said, holding my ground.

"You don't have a choice, little godling," Eli said as both his and Frankie's skin faded to matching shades of steel blue. Horns grew out of their heads. Even though they changed, they still had the same face shapes as Frankie and Eli. I cursed, stunned to see the darkbringer versions of my friends. But soon their faces narrowed, their cheeks moved higher. They appeared older now, like college kids.

I dropped my backpack and kicked it aside. "Where are my friends, my *real* friends?"

The fake Eli shrugged. "Probably dead."

I clenched my teeth so hard that my jaw hurt. Tears pricked in my eyes.

"Awww, is the little baby going to cry now?" Eli said, making sniffling noises.

A single tear rolled down my cheek. "Where has the Lord of Shadows taken my father?"

"Do you think we'd really tell you?" Eli said. "Lead *you* there?"

"When I'm done with you, you'll wish you had."

I spun the staff, and the symbols flashed a bright white, which only made the darkbringers madder. The fake Frankie sprouted wings and flew at me with outstretched claws. I jumped out of her way, but not fast enough — her razor-sharp nails raked my cheek. Papa's warning from the last time we practiced with staffs ran through my head. *Don't get too cocky.* Now my face was on fire and bleeding.

In the attack, I lost my footing and hit the ground hard enough to knock the wind from my lungs. Dirt stirred at

Eli's feet until it grew into a windstorm that headed straight for me. I climbed to my knees in time to flip the staff in front of my body before it hit. The staff inhaled the dirt, sucking it into the wood like a great whirlpool in the middle of the ocean.

I didn't have to direct the staff anymore. It was a part of me, an extension of myself, and I was an extension of it. I could feel my mind stretching and reaching beyond my body. My senses sharpened. Every sound around me amplified. I could smell the odor of the forest, the grass, and something more feral, like animal musk. But I could smell the Dark too, the tartness of the air. The tear in the veil burned my nose.

Before I got distracted by these new, deeper sensations, I sent the dirt back at Eli. It knocked him through the tear in the veil. I spun in time to block Frankie's claws, inches from my back. The force of her attack knocked me to the ground again.

When she came hurtling for me, her claws outstretched, I slammed the staff into her gut. Then I did something I wouldn't have believed in a thousand years. I lifted the darkbringer up on one end of the staff and threw her through the tear in the veil right into fake Eli. In the gloom of shadows inside the veil, I could barely make them out as they struggled to untangle themselves. I drew the staff across the tear and the fissure started to close.

"No!" the darkbringers screamed as they raced toward the closing rift, trying to get at me. Their outburst of magic struck me square in the chest and sent me flying backward. I hit the ground for the third time. But the darkbringers were too late. The tear had completely sealed, trapping them on the other side. I hoped there were no more tears nearby large enough to let them through. I'd find another way to save Papa.

TWENTY-TWO

I CATCH A BREAK

LYING ON MY BACK, I squeezed my eyes shut, and when I opened them again, Frankie and Eli stood over me frowning. The universe had to be getting a kick out of this. I banished two darkbringers who almost got the best of me, and *now* my friends decided to show up. If they were in fact my *real* friends this time.

"Are you okay?" Frankie asked, squinting at me.

I wasn't about to deal with more darkbringers and their games, so I asked, "Tell me how we know that dark matter exists."

She flinched. "What?"

My heart thundered against my chest. Only weeks ago, Eli had asked her the same question after she said he didn't have proof that ghosts were real. She hadn't hesitated to answer then, but now she looked perplexed. *Please don't let this be another trick.*

"Observable matter in the universe can't explain the motions of stars and galaxies." Frankie nudged up her glasses, which had slipped to the tip of her nose. "So scientists think there must be unobservable matter that's affecting gravitational forces."

I fought off the feeling of relief—not trusting it yet. "What's your favorite pie?"

"Pecan!" Frankie exclaimed. "But if it's the holidays, sweet potato!"

I blew out a breath. She was definitely Frankie. No doubt about it. "Eli, tell me your favorite ghost website of all time."

He frowned. "Maya, you're acting really weird."

I winced and bit the inside of my cheek. "Just *answer,* Eli."

"Well." He scratched his head. "Hands down, Ghost Sightings. They always have the most up-to-date theories, and Al and Carl Davis, the brothers who run the site, upload videos of their ghost hunting trips once a month and . . ."

My shoulders relaxed. "I needed to know that you were *my* friends and not imposters."

"Imposters?" Frankie said. "What did we miss?"

"Oh, just some darkbringers kicking my butt," I said as

they both stuck out a hand to help me up. I came to my feet and touched the place where the darkbringer had cut my face. It wasn't bleeding anymore. "Where were you guys?"

"Looking for you," Eli said. "We got knocked away from the staff and landed in the middle of the forest. We were starting to think you were stuck in the wormhole until we saw the lights. I guess it was the magic from your staff."

"Maya." Frankie's eyes were shiny and round with concern. "Are you okay?"

She didn't ask because of the half-healed cut on my face or the battle with the darkbringers. She meant was I okay that we'd gone into the Dark and left without rescuing my father. I couldn't answer, so I shook my head instead.

After catching up, we decided that we were in no shape to try to find a way back into the Dark until after we'd gotten some sleep. We laid out our sleeping bags between two trees under a tarp that Eli had brought for the trip. Frankie sat with her knees drawn against her chest and her arms wrapped around them. Eli was trying to get his phone to work, but his battery and backup battery had both gone dead in the Dark.

"This sucks!" He flung the phone onto his sleeping bag. "All I want to do is call Nana and check on Jayla. Is that too much to ask?"

I sat slouched over with my elbows digging into my knees. I missed Mama. She was probably worried sick and plenty mad. I felt bad that I hadn't left a note, but I *had* to do something. I'd admit this much: I should've come up with a halfway decent plan so I didn't almost get myself and my friends killed. The bright side: we were still alive. The not so bright side: so far we had failed.

"When are the other orishas going to come?" Eli threw up his arms in defeat. "I know the council said it takes time to cross the universe, but this is ridiculous."

"I agree." Frankie grimaced. "We need their help."

"Are you sure you're our Frankie and not a darkbringer?" Eli grinned. "Because *our* Frankie never agrees with me."

She poked out her tongue at him.

"We can't wait for the orishas to show up," I said, "but we do need a new plan."

"Starting with controlling our magic better," Frankie added.

My cheeks warmed as shame twisted my belly in knots. "You mean, you two. The best I can hope for is controlling the staff better."

Frankie stared as me wide-eyed. "Are you serious? You've been kicking darkbringers' butts with that staff. I think you may have opened that wormhole too."

Her tone was so direct that she might as well have been pointing a finger at my chest. I hadn't mastered all the powers of the staff. In fact, I didn't know the extent of its powers. I hadn't known that it was capable of repairing the veil, but it made sense now that I was thinking about it. Papa never left for work without it. I thought it was some silly tradition, but it was important to being a *guardian*.

"I suppose I could've opened the wormhole," I said, more to myself than to her. "The staff has a mind of its own. I don't always have to ask; sometimes it acts on my emotions or wants."

Frankie stared at Papa's staff with her nose scrunched up and *that look* again, but she bit her bottom lip.

Eli gulped in a deep breath. "When I turned invisible on the battlefield, I couldn't stop thinking about finding a place to hide." He paused, staring at his hands. "I couldn't stop thinking about that darkbringer in the helicopter either . . ."

In the worst of times, Eli always had a sense of humor —it was what got him through being scared even when we were little. Sometimes we had to face the thing bothering us. Sometimes it was easier to pretend that everything was okay. Like with him, it was getting harder for me to pretend.

"Eli . . ." I started, but I didn't know what to say to make him feel better.

"I'll take first watch!" he blurted out, cutting me off.

I didn't press him. I wasn't ready to talk about the accident either.

Eli may have volunteered for the watch, but he fell asleep

first. Sleep was like an infection. Frankie fell asleep not a full ten minutes after. I listened to my friends' soft snores, which were like a lullaby that made my eyes heavier. We were safe, and soon we would get Papa back. I couldn't let myself believe otherwise. I lay down, thinking that I would only close my eyes for a few minutes, but soon I was asleep too.

TWENTY-THREE

WHEN WE BECOME THE
MAIN COURSE FOR DINNER

I SLEPT LIKE A BABY until the sound of tiny bells slipped into my dreams. The bells made beautiful music that danced in my head and made me want to do anything to find the source. When my eyes flew open, I thought about the elokos. Papa said that they could enchant you by ringing little bells. My second thought was to cover my ears, but it was too late as I bolted up in my sleeping bag. Frankie was gone, and Eli was shuffling out of our tent with a goofy smile on his face.

No! I shouted in my head, but my legs only pitched forward, step after step.

Soon I was stomping through the forest with my friends on the way to becoming dinner. I tried to fight the compulsion to follow the bells. There were two warring wants — no, *needs*—inside me. First was the desire with all my heart to follow the bells, to find the beautiful music that made my soul dance. The feeling reminded me of my favorite family vacation, when we went to Florida and rented a hotel by the beach. I remembered being afraid that Papa would get called away for work, but he didn't, and the vacation was perfect.

At the same time a little alarm was going off in my head. It was enough to make the hairs stand up on the back of my neck, but not enough to snap me out of the trance.

Vines whipped around my ankles, stones dug into my bare feet, and I stubbed my big toes on tree roots as we marched deeper into the forest. It was the pain that snapped me out of my half-dreamy, half-awake state. But it didn't give me enough strength to break free.

Frankie, Eli, no! I screamed. *Don't listen to the bells.*

As much as I struggled to get the words out, only a whimper came from my lips. I tried to remember what Papa had done to escape the trance, but I couldn't get it straight in my head. The chiming bells were scrambling my thoughts.

Frankie was the first one who got a word out, although I wouldn't call it exactly coherent. "St . . . op . . . can't . . ." she stumbled. "Can't . . . sto . . ."

I got the point. We all did. Eli didn't say anything, but the erratic jerks in his shoulders meant that he was trying to escape too. The bells were so beautiful and serene that they drew my mind back to the memory of Florida. Back to the ocean. The beach. The warm sand. The pineapple slushies served in real pineapples. The best banana splits and mac and cheese in the world. The smell of warm fudge mixed with cold vanilla ice cream was so powerful that I smacked my lips. Somehow the bells were making me relive my favorite vacation to keep me in a trance.

When I snapped out of the daze this time, we were in a dense part of the forest where no stars or moonlight reached. We marched through the bushes in a straight line. The bells didn't just enchant us, they also painted a roadmap in our minds. I knew exactly where I was going, like I'd been there a hundred times before.

The smell of fish and salt on the air drew me back into my memory of our vacation in Florida. Papa and Mama lay in beach chairs next to each other. Mama was reading a book with a woman with a fancy dress on the cover, the sort of dress you only saw in movies. Papa flipped through a sports magazine. He was wearing another one of his bright, multicolored shirts, but for once, he fit in perfectly at the beach.

"Why don't you both come swimming?" I asked them in the memory.

"I'm coming, honey." Mama turned a page in her book. "Let me finish this chapter first."

I'd heard that yesterday too, and I didn't think a chapter took an hour to read, but that was how long it took her. Then when she came, it was only up to her waist because she didn't want to get her hair wet. Papa and I didn't care about getting our hair wet, though. We went deeper, and I wasn't afraid when he was with me.

"Did you know that the ocean was where Olodumare seeded humankind?" Papa said. "The universe wanted humans to one day evolve into a great species. And though humans have come far, there is much work to be done to realize the universe's true dream."

When I snapped out of the memory again, my world had turned upside down. The elokos had bound me between two trees—my feet to one tree and my wrists to another—like meat on a skewer. I craned my neck to see Frankie and Eli tied to trees too. The three of us were in netted hammocks filled with herbs.

I wriggled, but I couldn't get free. The ropes were too tight.

"Is this some sort of payback for talking too much?" Eli yelled to the sky. "Next time I'll keep my big mouth shut."

"The bells have stopped," I said, straining to hear over Eli's complaining.

The elokos were shorter than us, with green, scaly skin and a lot of teeth—a double row on the bottom for good measure. I swallowed hard when I saw them going about their business in the clearing. Bringing in firewood, scrubbing pots, crushing herbs into pastes. I couldn't help but think that they looked like really scary elves.

When one set a fire underneath Eli, he shouted, "Hey, don't be a jerk, let us go. You know cannibalism will get you jail time."

"They're technically not cannibals," Frankie said, "and you're not helping."

I still couldn't remember what my father said he'd done to free himself from the elokos in his story. And even worse, I was starting to feel dizzy from craning my neck to see them setting a fire beneath me.

"I don't suppose we can try reasoning with them?" Frankie asked.

"They don't seem like the reasoning type." Eli lifted his body up to gnaw at the thick vines that bound his hands. An eloko in a grass skirt swatted him with a stick. "Ouch," Eli yelped. "Is that any way to treat guests?"

"You mean guests they plan to eat," I said. "I doubt there's any etiquette for that."

"Well, there should be," Eli retorted. "They're rude!"

"I think they're telepathic," Frankie said, observing them like a hawk. Her glasses were lopsided but luckily hadn't fallen off. I wondered if the elokos knew that things like glasses and clothes were inedible. Or maybe they'd pick around them to get to the rest of the juicy meat. The thought turned my stomach. "None have said anything," she added, "so they have to be communicating through some other means. Mind to mind seems the most obvious."

I didn't care whether they were telepathic or not. It didn't matter. They were going to eat us, and I couldn't stop thinking about how I wanted things to go back to the way they used to be. Deep down, I knew that they never would. I had been so happy on our vacation in Florida, with not a care in the world. Now those days where gone, and I would never get them back. Papa had tried to warn me about this side of the world, and I wished I'd listened to him.

A song he used to sing to me popped into my head.

From the morning's glow to the evening's low
There's much work to do and many places to go
But no matter how far I travel or the people I see
There's nowhere in the whole world I'd rather be
For though I must fight to hold the beasts at bay
No mountain or storm or foe will keep me away
For I'll cross raging rivers and bend hyperspace
Just to see a smile on my sweet baby girl's face

The song. That was it. Papa had outwitted the elokos by singing.

"From the morning's glow to the evening's low," I sang

off-key. "There's much work to do and many places to go."

"Are you *singing?*" Frankie asked, still working to free her hands.

"Shhh," I hissed at her, then continued my off-key song, "But no matter how far I travel or the people I see, there's nowhere in the whole world I'd rather be."

It wasn't working. Some of the elokos shook their heads at me. Was my singing voice *that* bad? But it wasn't my imagination that the elokos stoked the fires and added more wood to speed up the process. They moved with the determination of creatures who'd done this a thousand times. How many hikers or campers had fallen into their trap over the years, or centuries, or millennia?

"Why isn't it working?" I said between gritted teeth.

"Why isn't what working?" Frankie said. "I'm so confused."

"The singing," Eli said. "You thought it would do something."

I told them about my father's run-in with the elokos and what he'd done to escape. "I don't understand why it isn't working for me."

"First, I've heard your father sing," Eli said. "He's got a voice out of this world, and well, I guess that it's because he is from *out of this world*. Must be an orisha thing. Maybe for the singing to work you need to . . ."

"Sing on key?" Frankie finished with a question.

My cheeks warmed, not as hot as my backside but close. I took a deep breath to calm my nerves and started again, slower this time, and not as far off-key: "For though I must fight to hold the beasts at bay, no mountain or storm or foe will keep me away, for I'll cross raging rivers and bend hyperspace just to see a smile on my sweet baby girl's face."

"That's kind of sweet," Eli cut in.

"Stop interrupting," Frankie said. "Let's try again together, Maya."

Because my friend was a genius, she'd learned the lyrics after hearing the song only once. We started together, singing from the beginning, slow at first, to make sure that our voices were in tune. The elokos slowed but didn't stop completely.

The fourth time through the song, Eli joined in and our voices synced, the melody on beat finally. We didn't sound half bad. We weren't good exactly, but we weren't first-round-singing-competition bad either. This time the elokos stopped cold. The ones who'd been in the middle of stooping down to put more wood on the fires froze in place. Some were bending over pots and pans, and it made me wonder where they had gotten dishes from. Had they enchanted some poor campers and taken their cookware as a parting gift?

As we kept singing, the three of us tried to wriggle our

way free. Whenever our voices were out of sync, the elokos twitched and gritted their teeth. My sweaty palms slipped on the rope as I worked my fingers between the tight knots.

Frankie loosened the rope around her wrists enough to unclasp her hands. Once she did, she flung a bolt of energy at the ground next to the fire beneath me. At first I didn't understand what she was doing, and I was more than a little annoyed when dirt splashed in my mouth. I spat out the dirt, but Frankie and Eli kept singing. And Eli had a little more amusement in his voice than I thought necessary.

Before I could tell her what a bad shot she was, I realized that she had perfect aim. Her magic had knocked a mound of dirt on top of the fire and put it out. Eli disappeared and became a disembodied voice. He sounded muffled, like he was eating, or . . . chewing at his ropes.

As I untied my hands, splashes of dirt landed on the fire underneath Frankie. Eli had freed himself. He faded back into physical form and helped Frankie down while I unraveled the rope around my ankles. Luckily, we weren't too far from the ground, and my feet landed on top of the smoking mound.

The elokos shook, but our song kept them frozen.

"I have an idea," Eli said, wiggling his eyebrows. "Let's eat them instead."

I could've sworn I saw tears swell in some of the elokos' eyes.

Frankie scooped up some loose rope. "I *am* hungry."

The eloko closest to me whimpered.

We weren't going to really eat them, but they didn't have to know that. There wasn't enough rope to tie them all up, but we tied up as many as we could.

"Serves you right," Eli said, leaning in close to one of the elokos. "Next time eat a salad."

The three of us ran back to camp, singing the entire time. When we arrived, I almost dropped to my knees. I stumbled over my feet, taking in the campsite with horror. Someone had ransacked our things. Cotton from our sleeping bags was everywhere. My backpack had been emptied and the contents scattered on the ground.

Frankie bent over, breathing hard like she was hyperventilating. "Crap."

I frantically searched the campsite up and down, my whole body shaking. But it was no use. Papa's staff was gone. I'd lost the one thing that he needed to repair the veil and keep the Lord of Shadows at bay. The one thing that could bring him home.

TWENTY-FOUR

I LEARN A NEW TRICK

FRANKIE, ELI, AND I lay our heads on one another's shoulders against a tree, half asleep. We had fought to stay awake all night, and my throat was sore from singing. The elokos' bells chiming in my dreams had jerked me awake at sunrise, and I felt groggy and confused. I reached for Papa's staff and grasped a handful of dry leaves and dirt. The memories flooded in as I stumbled to my feet. I swiped away the tear prickling my tired eyes. I could cry later; now I had to do something . . . *anything.*

I circled around the camp, looking for the staff again, hoping that we'd only missed it in the dark. It made no sense. The thieves hadn't taken our money or food. From what I could tell, the only things missing were the staff and

Eli's prods. I clutched my hands into fists and kicked at an empty water bottle lying on the ground.

"You think it was darkbringers?" Frankie asked from behind me.

I didn't answer. I didn't want to talk. I wanted to scream at the top of my lungs.

"Maya?" Frankie whispered. "It's going to be okay."

I spun around. "It's not going to be okay," I said, my voice trembling. "How are we going to stop the Lord of Shadows and the darkbringers? Maybe you think it's okay because you have magic, but for someone like me, a godling with no powers, how can I do anything to help without the staff?"

Frankie squeezed her lips tight and shook her head. She couldn't explain away hard facts with another one of her theories. Nothing would change the fact that the staff was gone and I'd failed my father. I'd failed everyone.

"What are you going to do?" she asked, raising her voice. "Are you going to give up because you don't have the staff? After all we've gone through, are you going to quit?"

Between the three of us, Frankie was always the most even-tempered and logical. So when she snapped, I was stunned, but I squared my shoulders and quickly recovered.

"Of course not!" I yelled back, giving her my meanest death stare. Eli jerked awake against the tree behind Frankie. His eyes stretched wide as he looked around for danger. "Did Oya quit all those times Dr. Z and his cronies had a new way to nullify her powers? No. Did Mama quit when she got transferred to the night shift and had to work ridiculous hours? No. Did Papa quit guarding the veil when he saw the first tear—"

"Okay, then." Frankie beamed at me. "Stop feeling sorry for yourself."

"It's not a good look," Eli said, coming up beside Frankie.

"What is this?" I threw up my arms in frustration. "An intervention?"

Frankie cocked her head to the side. "Do you need one?"

"You don't get it because you have magic," I said.

Frankie squinted at me. "I think you do too."

"What?" both Eli and I said.

Frankie adjusted her glasses. "I have a theory."

I moaned and glanced up to the treetops like they could save me from another one of her theories. I really wasn't in the mood, but all the energy had drained from my body like air leaving a balloon. There was no point in this argument, and we were wasting time. As soon as I could find a tear in the veil, I was going back into the Dark, staff or no staff, to save my father.

"This isn't the time," Eli muttered under his breath. "Not everything requires a *theory*."

"There's where you're wrong *again*, Eli," Frankie snapped at him too. She really was on a roll, and despite being mad,

I liked seeing this side of her. My friend with the highest IQ of our school, straight-A student, and biggest science nerd in history. Without her and Eli at my side these past few days, I didn't know where I'd be. "There's always time for science."

"You're exaggerating now," Eli said with a dismissive wave.

When Frankie shot her own death stare at him, he instantly stopped talking. She turned back to me, daring me to say anything else to interrupt her. With that look, I wasn't about to make the same mistake.

"I think the staff is a conduit," she said. "Like a channel to carry something from one place to another."

"What's your point, Frankie?" I asked, impatient.

"What if the staff doesn't have any magic on its own?" she said, after biting her lip. "What if its actual function is to help you channel your own magic? That would mean that you do have magic after all, and the staff only amplifies it."

"That's a great theory *in theory*," I said, pleased with my play on words. "But the reality is that without the staff, I have no magic. When you two were in danger, your magic showed. We were about to be eaten by elokos, and I couldn't do anything to help us escape but sing."

"Think about it, Maya," Frankie begged, and she might as well have said, *Be logical for once.* "None of the darkbringers can open a wormhole into the human world; it's a rule of the veil so they can't get out. The only reason they've been able to escape is through the tears. So that means one of us had to create the wormhole that saved our butts from the darkbringer army."

"It wasn't me," Eli said. "I didn't even know what a wormhole was until you told me."

"My magic is energy-based," Frankie added. "I can manipulate it, shape it, and use it as a shield or a weapon. You see now?" When I didn't answer, she added, "It wasn't possible for Eli or me to create the wormhole because that's not what our magic does."

I remembered the night I followed Papa in our neighborhood and he disappeared. One minute he was walking on the street not too far ahead of me, and then he turned the corner and was gone. At the time, I thought the shadows had swallowed him. Now I knew what my father was capable of, or at least a fraction of it. The orishas were powerful and ancient, and I had a feeling that there was a lot more about them that I didn't know or understand. Maybe there was a lot more about myself I didn't know too.

"Don't you think if I could open my own personal gateway into the Dark, I would've gone back as soon as I could?" I sucked in a deep breath. My whole body was trembling. I was trying to not be too mad at Frankie. She meant well.

"Try to open a wormhole into the Dark," she demanded, crossing her arms.

"What?" I laughed so loud that the birds in a tree nearby flew away. "We're wasting time. I need to find a tear."

"She's right," Eli said. I eased out a sigh of relief because I thought he was agreeing with me until he added, "You should try, Maya."

They stood there staring at me like I was going to pull a trick from up my sleeve. Both of them made it sound as easy as getting on a bike and pedaling. Sure, you'd fall down a few times, scrape your knee or elbow, but eventually you'd get the hang of it. But this was different. I *had* tried. Well, not particularly to open up a wormhole, but I'd tried to reach deep inside myself with my mind to see if I had any magic.

The orisha council said that very few godlings even showed powers. Big help that was. It meant that you could possibly live your whole life waiting for them to come. Maybe they'd come when you were a baby or working the dreadful nine to five, or when you were old and on your deathbed. A hundred-year-old godling was still a young hatchling compared to an orisha.

Hatchling.

Papa had called me that once with a goofy smile on his face. I would try for him.

Heat billowed under my skin. I thought my blood

pressure was high, which happened with my anemia, but this was something else.

I'd felt the same heat when the shadows attacked me in our neighborhood and at every scrape of danger. I hadn't thought much of it. *My skin feels hot* wasn't the most interesting conversation starter, and it didn't seem relevant.

"Okay, I'll try," I said, giving in. It couldn't hurt, could it?

Eli bounced on his toes in excitement, and Frankie nudged his shoulder to stop. I turned away from my friends and faced a pine tree.

Heat pricked in my fingertips like needlepoints, and sweat beaded on my forehead. It was still early in the day, and it was already hot, but I could feel something else building up inside me. Something waking, *a force;* okay, maybe that wasn't the right word to describe it. It was something, though, something that boiled in my blood. I tilted my head forward a bit as my field of vision narrowed to a very small point in front of me. I could no longer see Frankie or Eli out of the corner of my eyes, or anything else for that matter. There was only the spot halfway between the tree and me.

A spark of light fluttered in front of the tree. Sweat streaked down my forehead now, but I couldn't break my concentration to wipe it away. Something was happening. It felt like trying to remember a dream that you'd forgotten, having it on the edge of your mind just out of reach. The spark sputtered and went out. I drew in a shaky breath.

Instead of feeling discouraged, I turned to my friends, who were grinning at me.

"Did you see that?" I pointed at the empty spot. "I did that. I made that spark happen."

"Give it another try," Frankie said, her face smug.

I turned to the tree again. Not only did my friends and the tree and the entire forest fade to the background, they faded to black. Everything around me outside of that one spark of light became an afterthought in my mind. The spark didn't sputter this time. It grew and grew. It wasn't like the tears in the veil that looked like a jagged line cut with a dull knife. The spark grew into a black hole with a silver bridge made of glowing god symbols that lit our way into the Dark.

TWENTY-FIVE

SOMETHING BAD IS ABOUT TO HAPPEN

FRANKIE AND ELI slapped me on the shoulder, and my surroundings came back into focus. This time, I didn't lose the wormhole when my concentration broke. My friends were beaming at me, and my cheeks warmed in embarrassment. If it wasn't for them, I might have never tried to open a gateway at all.

Every kid should be so lucky to have friends who believe in you even when you don't believe in yourself. Friends who accept you exactly the way you are and help you be brave when you don't know that you can.

As we stood amazed by the wormhole, I realized that I couldn't ask them to go back into the Dark with me. Eli had his little sister, Jayla, to watch out for and Nana and

bingo night. Frankie was a science genius who could someday cure every problem in the human world if she put her
mind to it. Eshu, Oshun, and the rest of the council had
called *me* future guardian of the veil. That meant that I
had to protect our world from the Dark, starting with my
own family. Besides, Frankie had almost died there *twice:*
first with the poison, then Nulan. I couldn't put them at
risk again.

"Guys," I said, my voice small, "I have to do this alone."

Eli cocked an eyebrow and looked at Frankie. "Is she
trying to leave us behind and take all the credit for saving
the world?"

"Technically, her father would be saving the world; we're
saving him," Frankie said. "But yes, she's *totally* trying to be
the epic heroine alone, and we're not having it."

"We're coming"—Eli rolled his eyes—"and that's the
end of that."

"I really don't think that would be a good idea," I said.
"What if something happens—"

"Stop trying to do everything on your own, Maya,"
Frankie begged.

"You need us, and we want to help," Eli said, taking on
a serious tone. "Let us."

Eli and Frankie stared at me with their eyes narrowed
and their jaws set into matching scowls. If their godling
magic had been laser beams, I would've been in trouble,

because their death stare game had reached a new level. I was about to face my worst fears again, and I laughed so hard that I got a cramp in my side. Tears ran down my face. I couldn't have asked for better friends. They always had my back. But not all the tears were happy tears. No matter how strong I pretended to be, I was scared too. I gave in because Frankie and Eli were right (no surprise). I needed their help, and deep down I didn't want to face the Lord of Shadows alone.

"Huddle time." Eli spoke in his best coach impression, which was to say he sounded like he had a mouth full of cotton. "Bring it in."

And we did. We stood in a circle with our heads together and our arms draped across each other's shoulders. "I don't mean to be the one to say this," Frankie said, wrinkling her nose, "but we smell pretty bad."

"That's the fresh scent of the League of Godlings." Eli stuck out his chin. "No true hero or heroine smells good after saving the world."

"Technically, we haven't saved—" Frankie said.

"We need to go before I lose the wormhole," I said, interrupting their usual bickering. "Or before some darkbringer on the other side decides to come through. We need a plan."

"We have a plan," Eli said. "Kick darkbringers' butts and save your father."

"Maya's saying that we need a *strategy*," Frankie said. "She's right."

"Yes, that's exactly what I mean," I said, playing along when I hadn't even thought about a strategy until now. "When I was opening the wormhole, I concentrated on a place close to my father but safe for us to enter the Dark. Our best bet is to search for him undetected. For that, we need stealth."

Eli's eyes lit up, and he grinned. "Or invisibility."

With that, we hatched out our strategy, which wasn't foolproof or particularly clever. It was simple: sneak into the Dark while invisible, avoid the darkbringers, find the epicenter, and get my father out. We gathered what little we could salvage of our gear and food into Frankie's backpack. Then we stood in front of the wormhole side by side, staring into the black tunnel that would take us back into the Dark. My heart raced, and my teeth chattered. "Ready?" I asked, pushing down my fears.

"Ready," Eli and Frankie said, as nervous as me.

Eli stood between the two of us and reached for our hands. "It'll be easier to keep you invisible during the trip if we stay connected."

"We don't mind holding your hand to make sure you don't get lost," I teased him.

"I do." Frankie grimaced. "Your hand is so sweaty."

"Yours is too," Eli shot back.

"I know," Frankie said with a shrug.

As we walked into the wormhole, wind whipped around our feet and flung us forward. The first wormhole I made was like hanging upside down on a roller coaster. This one was like climbing into an elevator that traveled at the speed of light.

"It's coming to an end," I said, feeling the Dark near. "Get ready, it's going to be bumpy."

Eli squeezed my hand and must've done the same to Frankie because she said, "Ouch."

We shot out of the wormhole fast, and the velocity wrenched us apart. I hit the ground. "Ugh," I groaned as the impact knocked the wind from my lungs. The brooding slate-blue sky of the Dark and white particles swam across my vision. It was night here again.

"Sorry," I said when I saw my friends lying on the ground too. They grumbled and rolled on their backs. "Looks like I still have some work to do on my speed and velocity."

"I don't think we're invisible anymore," Frankie said, staring at her hand.

"I lost my concentration," Eli said as we sat up, nursing our bumps and bruises.

We were in a field with crunchy dead grass poking our backsides.

The wormhole roared in our ears, but my attention

was on the ring of small buildings not even a hundred feet away.

"Are we in the right place?" Eli asked, looking at the distant town too.

"Yes," I said, my belly twisting into knots. "He's close."

"Um, Maya, what are you going to do about that wormhole?" Frankie cleared her throat and glanced over her shoulder.

When I turned around, my mouth fell open. The wormhole was a huge ball of spinning gray dust like a tornado lying on its side. I had expected it to close by itself like my first accidental wormhole, but it didn't. Now it was basically a neon sign saying ENTER THE HUMAN WORLD HERE.

My father had come and gone from the Dark undetected forever, so there had to be a way for me to do it too. When I concentrated, the wormhole sparked around the edges and started to shrink. Frankie spotted a flock of darkbringers flying straight for us. Sure, blue people with horns and barbed tails were scary. But blue people with horns and barbed tails armed with battleaxes flying straight at you, that was a new kind of terror.

Eli stretched his invisibility over us while I worked on collapsing the wormhole. I was happy to inherit my father's ability to enter the Dark, but it wasn't the most useful power to have in a fight. I missed the staff.

"Can you go any faster?" Frankie nudged.

"Going as fast as I can," I said through gritted teeth. I was sweating buckets. Opening and closing wormholes was harder than it looked, and my powers were exhausted. "This is pretty much rocket science."

Frankie looked skyward again. "I'd say we have less than a minute."

"I count fourteen of them." Eli grimaced. "That aziza general—the one who looks like a fairy—is leading them."

"You mean Commander Nulan," Frankie said, her voice full of the same dread I felt.

Not her again. Anyone but her. She may have been one of the beautiful aziza, but she was ruthless. I still couldn't believe she killed one of her own soldiers. She'd almost killed Frankie too and would have no qualms about trying again. I couldn't let her get through the gateway to hurt more people.

Eli stood with his hands balled into fists, staring up at the darkbringers. The whooshing sound of their wingbeats rivaled the roar of the wormhole. It was a foreshadowing of the danger to come.

Sparks danced on Frankie's fingertips. "I'll slow them down."

"I . . . just . . . need . . . a few more minutes," I said as she raised her hands skyward. I could feel the vibrations in the wormhole, feel it close inch by inch. A few more minutes. Three at best, but we were out of time.

Flashes of light crackling like electricity shot out of Frankie's hands. The air around us rippled as her magic tore through the sky. The darkbringers broke their flight path to get out of the way. Most moved in time, but two of them got caught in her blast and spiraled out of control.

Eli slapped Frankie on the back. "Nice shot! Only twelve more to go!"

We had no time to celebrate as the darkbringers paired off into smaller groups. While the rest circled above the wormhole, one group attacked. They raised their arms and blew fireballs in our general direction. Their aim was way off because Eli's magic still held and they couldn't see us.

Frankie sent another blast, knocking the fire-breathing darkbringers to the ground. "Take that, you bullies!"

But as soon as she said it, Nulan sent a knife straight through Frankie's shoulder. I gasped as my friend stumbled and the blade entered the wormhole. "There you are, little godlings," came Commander Nulan's sickly sweet voice.

She swooped down and landed twenty feet away. We were still invisible, but she didn't need to see us to figure out our position. She'd guessed at least one of us would cover the wormhole, and she must've heard us talking.

"Are you okay?" I whispered, staring at Frankie's wound, which looked particularly ghastly in her semitransparent state. Eli tore a piece of his T-shirt and tied it around the cut.

"Is the wormhole closing on its own?" Frankie answered my question with a question. When I nodded, she sighed. "It looks smaller."

She was right. I could sense the gateway shrinking, but at a snail's pace.

"We need to protect it until the end so no darkbringers get through," she said quietly so Nulan wouldn't hear us.

"*We* . . . yes," I said, confused. "Isn't that what we're doing?"

"So you were foolish enough to come back?" Nulan asked, her eyebrow raised, as she crept closer. "You weak, pathetic little children."

I gritted my teeth and squeezed my hands into fists. Maybe I didn't have any powers to blast her to pieces, but I could still give her a black eye.

"I'm going to stay to protect the wormhole," Frankie said, her face determined. "Go save your father while I keep Nulan occupied."

"No," I whispered, feeling numb inside. "I can't leave you."

Frankie set her jaw as the other darkbringers landed in a circle around us. "Go now before we're all trapped here."

Without waiting for us to argue over it, Eli released Frankie from his invisibility magic. The last of it shimmered against her skin before she became solid again. Commander Nulan's eyes landed on Frankie, and she curled her lips into a devious smile. "Did your friends leave you alone to defend the wormhole, little godling?" Nulan sneered. "What a horrible mistake. Like I said before, I don't have any qualms about killing you."

Frankie shifted her position into a wide stance, magic sparking on her fingertips. She stood between Nulan and the wormhole. "Go," she whispered to us, then to Nulan she said, her voice shaking, "It only takes one godling to stop you."

"Come on." Eli dragged me away, tears in his eyes. "Don't let her sacrifice be for nothing."

Her sacrifice—no, she couldn't. I started to pull away, but then I stopped. Frankie was backing toward the mouth of the wormhole. She could enter it before it closed and go home if she timed it right. And Frankie would've already run the calculations in her head.

Eli and I ran, and the roar of the wormhole masked our footsteps. We didn't stop until we were clear of the darkbringers closing in on Frankie. When we stopped, my breath seized in my chest. Frankie was surrounded. There was no way she could fend off all those darkbringers. I made a step to run back, but Eli grabbed my shoulder to stop me.

"You have to keep going, Maya"—Eli chewed on his lip —"while there's still a chance."

"Then you help her," I said. "I'll be okay on my own from here."

"But . . ." Eli looked back and forth between Frankie and me. "I want to help you both."

"You have." I backed away from him. "You gave me a head start on Nulan."

I took off at a sprint, running straight for the epicenter. I'd only taken a few steps when I felt his magic fade against my skin. I turned back to normal.

By the time I reached the edge of the city, Frankie yelled, "You're going to totally regret that!"

I pushed back tears, knowing that I had left my friends to fight for their lives alone, when they never left me behind. Not even once.

TWENTY-SIX

I FIND SOMETHING UNEXPECTED

I **BARRELED THROUGH THE DEAD GRASS** toward the epicenter. Sweat stung my eyes, and my legs ached. I felt like a jerk for leaving my friends in trouble like that, especially after all we'd been through together. I wanted to go back, but Eli was right. Frankie and he had risked their lives so that I could get a head start on Nulan. I couldn't waste it or my chance to save my father.

Heat simmered under my skin when I thought about the commander. She was as bloodthirsty as the Lord of Shadows himself. The way she talked about my father like he was nothing more than a fly to swat made me even angrier. Did every single darkbringer truly understand what the Lord of Shadows was planning? I thought about the kids we saw on the edge of the cornfield and the endless farms we passed trying to find my father. There were regular people here, not in the army and not bloodthirsty like Nulan. Did they know that the Lord of Shadows wanted to kill all humans and orishas and godlings? He wanted total annihilation, and he'd stop at nothing to get it. How could anyone go along with something so vile?

Hate was number one on Mama's list of complicated emotions, along with envy, anger, and shame. She'd said that all emotions fell somewhere on the *complicated scale*. It wasn't rocket science to figure out that hate could grow into something more dangerous. Imagine having a pet monster that you fed every day. It would grow stronger and eventually eat you alive. That was how hate worked. It was a monster that consumed you until (plot twist), you became the monster. I didn't want to become a monster, but I was really starting to hate the Lord of Shadows. But unlike him, I didn't want to destroy all the people in the Dark. I only wanted to stop them from destroying us.

I could feel Papa's presence stronger now that I was at the edge of town. My heart raced against my chest, and I wiped my sweaty hands on my pants, which were all kinds of dirty already. A dark mist shrouded the town, but I could see that nothing was moving inside. No traffic or people talking, no hum of electricity in the air, no birds chirping. No sound at all.

I'd read enough comics to know that I was walking

into a trap. The Lord of Shadows hadn't even tried to be clever about it. I guessed that was his style, or most likely he wanted to taunt me like he'd done on the crossroads. He was dangerous then and even more dangerous now.

When I stepped closer to the epicenter, I saw the weirdest thing. Streets ended at the edge of the dead grass like it was normal for roads to stop in the middle of nowhere. Power lines that looped from one pole to another cut off where the grass met the asphalt too. Half cords stood rigid in the air, held by something other than gravity. It looked like someone had cut out a piece of a city and plopped it down here. If the rest of the Dark was bluish in tint, this town was gray as ashes.

A stitch caught in my side and I stopped in my tracks, finally realizing the horrible truth. This was an exact copy of my neighborhood. Only, it looked like my dream on the crossroads when the Lord of Shadows drained the color from it. I sucked in a deep breath. It wasn't real. He made this illusion to taunt me because he knew my biggest fear was to lose my family and friends.

Everything I loved about home, about Chicago, about my life was wrapped up in my neighborhood. Mama and Papa, the cranky Miss Ida and Miss Lucille. Frankie and Eli, even my math teacher, Ms. Vanderbilt. I balled my hands into fists at my sides and headed for school.

"Get in, get my father, and get out," I whispered, blinking back tears. That was the plan.

On the way to my block, I rushed past the alley where Frankie and I had almost got eaten by werehyenas. Then I passed by the empty snow cone stand and the abandoned elotes cart. This time no sweet smell of roasted corn and butter and chili rolled up my nose. The two- and three-story greystone houses faced down each other like an old-fashioned duel. All the colors that made each house unique and the neighborhood feel alive were gone. The blue shutters on the Robinsons' windows. The yellow birdhouse in the Lewises' yard. The rusty red bike with the white basket Lakesha tied to the tree in front of her house and called *art*. Even the perfectly manicured grass that the cranky Johnston twins kept in order was dead. The purple and green Oya curtains at my window. It was all gray in this place, not a spot of color anywhere.

I crossed Ashland Avenue at a run. Cars sat in traffic frozen in time, gray down to their rubber tires that should've been black. There were no people in them and no sounds. This place gave new meaning to the term *ghost town*.

At Jackson Middle, a neon-green sign crackled off and on announcing that the Jaguars were regional soccer champions. The electricity left a sting in the air that smelled like hot metal. It was the only bit of color in this whole place.

Even though there was no breeze, the Jaguars flag at the top of the pole flapped around frantically. I glanced north of the soccer field toward the cafeteria. I kept thinking that any minute now darkbringers were going to burst out of it and attack.

My heart thundered against my chest when I crept up the steps to the gray double doors. The real Jackson Middle had red doors to the main building. I paused with my hand on the knob, listening again. The flag flapping in the wind was the only sound. There was no turning back, and I wouldn't even if I could. I had to do this for my father. I couldn't be the future guardian of the veil if I chickened out when something scared me.

"For Papa," I said aloud as I pushed open the door.

Shadows flickered across the half-lit hallway, but I sucked in a deep breath. My sneakers squeaked against the floor, and the hairs stood up on the back of my neck. All the classroom doors were closed, and the shadows seemed to writhe and lash out at me. It was only a short walk before I reached Ms. Vanderbilt's classroom. I glanced around the hallway again — expecting something to happen. When nothing did, I pressed my face up close to the glass in the door and peered inside. All the desks sat in perfect rows with a sheet of paper on each. It was just like in our world, where Ms. Vanderbilt always had pop quizzes ready at the beginning of class.

Bracing for an ambush, I rushed into the room, holding my breath. But it was completely empty. I stood in the middle of the room, turning in circles, tears pricking my eyes. Papa wasn't here. How could this be? I stared at the chalkboard. It had the ingredients for making candy apples, like on the day the world turned gray.

On the crossroads, the Lord of Shadows said that my father was at the epicenter of where it all began for me.

"But this *is* the epicenter," I said, my voice weak.

The clock on the wall ticked, and I jumped. It wasn't my imagination either that the shadows in the corners crawled closer. A thousand thoughts went through my head, and none of them made any sense. I wanted to outright cry instead of swiping at the tears on my cheeks. But I had to figure this out for Papa.

Again the Lord of Shadows' words replayed in my head.

The epicenter of where it all began for you.

"It began here!" I screamed. "Here!"

My voice echoed in the room.

Here, it mocked me. *Here.*

I stepped closer to the chalkboard, trying to remember the exact moment the world turned gray. Then I remembered something else. A week before that day in Ms. Vanderbilt's class, I'd seen a crack in the ceiling in the gym. Not a regular crack. It'd looked like crooked black lightning. At the time, we'd been doing breathing exercises on the mats, and I thought I had fallen asleep.

A tear in the veil.

I jetted from the room and down the hall. "The gym!"

My nerves were on edge, and my legs shook as I ran out of the main building and across the soccer field to reach the gym. I pushed open the double doors that were as creaky as the ones at the *real* Jackson Middle. I hurried down the hallway of awards and trophies behind glass walls, and then as soon as I stepped in the gym, I saw him.

"Papa!" I screamed.

I ran without thinking. Papa sat in a chair in the middle of the basketball court with his arms tied behind his back. His head and shoulders slumped forward, his back hunched over. Shadows moved in the gym, and there was only a little light coming from the windows.

My vision was a blur of tears as I fumbled with the rope that bound his hands. I noticed that it hadn't been all that tight, and he could have wiggled them loose on his own. That was another detail to taunt me. It wasn't the rope that had trapped my father here; it was something more powerful.

When I moved in front of Papa, he finally raised his head, his locs falling over his eyes. He looked confused, like he'd just woken from a long nap, but that look soon turned to shock and horror. "No, no, no," he whispered. "Maya, baby girl, you can't be here. It's a trap."

"I know, Papa." I bit my lip. "I had to help."

Tears streamed down my father's face too. "You shouldn't have come."

My mouth fell open. His words stung. I'd gone through so much to be here, and he needed my help. On top of that, I felt really bad for leaving Frankie and Eli behind to protect the wormhole and fight Nulan. "But I had to come."

"He took everyone I loved before," Papa said, his voice choked. "I couldn't protect them."

"I know, Papa." I knelt before him. In his stories, he was always the hero, but even heroes suffered. There was always a cost. Sometimes they suffered in small ways and sometimes in huge ways. Papa had made a mistake when he separated the human world from the Dark. When he created the veil, it hurt a lot of darkbringers—many died. Even though he'd fixed it, the Lord of Shadows couldn't forgive him for the damage he'd caused. Now I saw the regret burning in Papa's eyes. He looked smaller somehow, less heroic and more human. "We can stop him together," I said. "You and me."

"You're very brave, Maya." He smiled up at me. "Braver than you even know."

"Papa." I knotted my knuckles against my thighs. "I lost your magic staff."

For a moment he didn't say anything as he stared at me. His face was so tired. "Well, someone stole it," I added. "I'm sorry I couldn't take better care of it."

"Maya, honey." Papa frowned. "There's no magic in the staff."

"I know that now," I mouthed. I hadn't had time to really think about it since making the wormhole to get into the Dark. It was my magic that hit the darkbringers with so much force that it knocked them clear across a room. It helped us understand their language. It healed our wounds. *My magic.* "But that was your favorite staff."

Papa beamed at me, shaking his head, a little of his old self again. "I'll make a new one."

"We better go," I said, sensing the darkbringers near.

"I can't create a gateway." Papa's shoulders dropped. "I'm not sure how, but the Lord of Shadows has done something to block my ability to connect to the veil . . . I think it may be temporary . . . I'll know once I return to the human world."

"I can," I said, grinning up at him.

"That's my girl." He laughed, but his smile faded when the darkbringers started to pour into both entrances of the gym. He narrowed his eyes as he lifted his arm out and a staff identical to the one I lost appeared in his hand. I wanted one too, and Papa must have seen it on my face because he conjured another one.

"We need to get out now, Maya," Papa said. "How fast can you open a gateway?"

Not fast enough, I thought as the darkbringers lined up on either side of us, blocking the two sets of double doors. Commander Nulan stepped forward wearing her usual twisted grin.

"Congratulations, Maya." Her face turned into a nasty taunt. "You found your father. Now you will die with him."

I cringed at how I'd left Frankie and Eli to fight her and a dozen darkbringers. Now Nulan had five times as many soldiers with her. "My friends . . ." I said, my voice small.

"Oh, we don't have to worry about them anymore." Nulan smiled again. "I've taken care of that problem."

Sweat trickled down my back. *Taken care of that problem.* No, she couldn't have. My friends couldn't be gone. I couldn't trust anything she said. Frankie had a plan to get back through the wormhole, didn't she?

"You shame the aziza people, Nulan." Papa spat her name like there was history between them. A long, dark history. "How could you abandon them, or have you forgotten that your people live in the human world too?"

Nulan laughed, and her voice was like thunder crackling in the gym. "No more shamed than when Lutanga ran away and married you. What good came of that? She and your children died very slow and painful deaths."

If she was trying to anger Papa, it worked. His whole

body began to glow. But it wasn't my father who struck out at Nulan. I knocked my staff against the gym floor, and a streak of white light shot out. It hit Nulan so hard that she slammed into the line of darkbringers standing behind her. They crumpled to the floor in a heap.

Nulan shoved darkbringers out of her away and climbed to her feet again. Her curly hair stood up every which way and was smoking. She gritted her teeth, and her whole body shook.

Papa turned to me wide-eyed, his face gray. "Maya, the wormhole."

But there was no time.

"You'll pay for that!" Nulan screamed, and the darkbringers attacked.

Twenty-seven

The end of the road

Papa and I stood back-to-back, our staffs twisting as we struck darkbringer after darkbringer. They poured in through the doors on either side of the gym. I ducked to miss a club aimed straight for my face. Before the darkbringer could swing again, I cracked the staff against her knees. When she dropped to the ground, I landed another thrash across her head, knocking her out cold. She was going to wake up with the worst headache ever in a few hours.

Three darkbringers swung their battleaxes, and I thrust out the staff to catch the blows. They were much bigger than me, and I stumbled and almost lost my footing. But I remembered the moves Papa taught me, and instead of falling, I shifted my weight and spun left. That put a foot between me and the darkbringers. I flung out the staff in a wide arc, sending a wave of energy that rippled the space between me and them. Then one after another, the darkbringers disappeared. I stumbled back again, but this time from shock. I looked down at my hands, and the symbols on the black staff glowed as they rearranged themselves.

Papa was too busy dispatching darkbringers with his identical staff to notice. He broke legs and arms and noses, but none of them disappeared or, even worse, died. I'd seen what the orishas could do when the darkbringers attacked our neighborhood. Papa was holding back — keeping them at bay but not killing them. And I thought I understood why. He didn't want more lives lost because of a senseless feud between him and the Lord of Shadows. So if I made those darkbringers disappear, then what happened to them?

I didn't have time to think as something as slippery as a snake lashed around my waist and jerked me backwards. My staff fell and hit the floor, then the thing lifted me up high in the air. I clawed at what turned out to be a darkbringer's tail. It was thick like a rope. As the barb drove toward my heart, I grabbed the darkbringer's tail, stopping it from striking. I tried with all my might to conjure up my magic without the staff, but it was impossible. Yes, I felt the heat inside me growing hotter, but I couldn't make it do anything. The staff was a conduit, like Frankie said. Maybe it would be something I could learn to control with practice. That was if I lived long enough.

The tail slammed me to the ground, and pain shot through my body. I cried out as my vision went blurry. There were two Papas and too many darkbringers to count. The impact knocked the wind out of me too, and I struggled to get up.

Papa screamed, and the slippery tail turned into ash and so did the darkbringer it belonged to. Finally when my head cleared, I climbed to my feet. Papa hadn't only killed that darkbringer; he'd turned *them all* into ash. Every single darkbringer in the gym. I couldn't breathe as the new silence echoed in the space. There was no sound except for my heavy breathing.

A brown face and wild hair poked around the edge of the doorway, and my heart slammed against my chest. Nulan had somehow gotten away before my father turned the darkbringers into ash. When our eyes met, she sneered at me and slinked back into the dark like the coward she was. Papa stood there shaking and had to brace himself against the wall under the basketball rim. He'd killed them. *Killed them all.* If I hadn't truly understood what was at stake before, I did now. Dread washed over me, and I felt like throwing up. I wrapped my arm around my belly as I walked over to him. Papa shook his head, his eyes wide and filled with soft white light. We'd won, but at what cost? Dozens of darkbringers had died in an instant.

"I didn't want to do that," Papa said, his voice streaked with pain. "If we keep fighting, it won't make things better. The Lord of Shadows won't stop until he's driven both worlds to extinction. You don't know what it was like before. So many deaths. If I don't stop the veil from failing, it will happen again."

"It won't happen if we work together, Papa," I said, my voice rising. He had to stop treating me like a little kid. "I can help you guard the veil."

Papa patted the top of my head and smiled, his face sad. He tried to hide it, but his magic was completely drained. He couldn't even stand without leaning against the wall.

"Maya, open a wormhole," he said, half out of breath. "I need to get back to the human world to be able to heal, and we need to get you to safety."

I thought about my friends as I turned to an empty space on the back wall. *They had to be okay.* My fists shook as the first sparks came to life. The wormhole was growing slower than the one I made in the forest, and I could tell that my magic was exhausted too. It would take too long on my own, so I retrieved the staff to help conduct my magic. I drew a line in the air that looked like crooked black lightning. That was the first step; now I had to make the tear grow into a wormhole. But what if I couldn't close it once we got to the other side like before? I couldn't let that fear get the best of me. Instead, I concentrated on opening the wormhole in our neighborhood. I picked right in front of the cranky twins' house, knowing that they would be the first on the scene to help if we needed it.

I tried hard, but it wasn't growing fast enough. My father put a hand on my shoulder and squeezed. I looked up at him, and he was beaming again. "No more secrets, okay?" I said, setting my jaw so he knew I meant it. No more me hiding things like I'd done with the cracks in the veil and the writhing shadows. No more him trying to protect me from knowing about the dangers of his job. Besides, I was going to be a guardian of the veil one day too.

"No more secrets," he repeated.

"Okay," I said, turning back to the sputtering spark.

The wormhole was growing but taking its sweet time, which was to say, it was so slow that I thought I would age a year before it was large enough for us to fit.

I jumped when the doors slammed shut on both sides of the gym. A warm white light spread across the basketball court, and the walls, windows, and doors glowed.

"Are more darkbringers coming?" I asked, heart racing.

"No," Papa said, his face somber. "*He's* coming."

There was an unmistakable edge of panic in my father's voice.

The Lord of Shadows was coming.

Crap.

TWENTY-EIGHT

THE LORD OF SHADOWS LIVES
UP TO HIS REPUTATION

A CHILL RAN DOWN MY BACK. *He* was coming. I could feel the Lord of Shadows' presence like a cloud that had blocked out the sun, or a sudden chill on a warm day. Papa's magic shimmered against the walls. He had cast a sort of net that was a smaller version of the veil, but he looked even worse. His eyelids fluttered, and sweat poured down his forehead. He looked like he would collapse from exhaustion any minute.

"It won't keep him out long," Papa said, "but it should give us more time."

More time. His words ran circles in my mind, and my head throbbed like a toothache from focusing so hard. This guardian thing wasn't easy. I didn't know how Papa had done it all these years, all these *eons*. He'd come and gone between worlds, repaired the veil, and kept another war from happening. I squared my shoulders. If he could do that, then I could open this wormhole. My life depended on it. Papa's. My friends'. Mama's. The cranky orisha twins'. Everyone's.

The wormhole grew and grew, a little faster now. My vision narrowed until the rest of the world faded to black. The spark stopped sputtering around the edges just as the gym began to shake. It made my teeth clatter together.

Darkness darker than the blackest night fell in the room. If it hadn't been for Papa's miniveil, which was shrinking each second, it would have been completely dark. The temperature dropped fast, and frost shot across the windows and up the walls. I held my breath as the frost spread through the protection net.

"Maya, no matter what happens," Papa said, his voice a whisper, "I want you to go through the gateway as soon as it's stable. Promise me that you will, even if I'm not with you."

"But, Papa!" I yelled as wind whipped from the wormhole and sparks flashed inside it. It was almost stable.

"No *buts*, Maya," Papa said, his voice firm. "I'll hold him off as long as possible while you escape."

I squeezed my lips together to keep from protesting again, and as soon as I did, the doors flew open on one side of the gym. A gust of cold air slammed into me, and I couldn't breathe. *It was him.* His presence sucked up the space in the room like he was bigger than the gym itself. Speaking of which, the gym grew wider and taller until it was the size of a football field.

The Lord of Shadows' writhing purple and black ribbons snaked into the gym first. They slinked across the floor like pet vipers seeking mice to snack on. A dozen, then hundreds of them, crawling up the walls, slithering on the basketball rim. Fear froze me in place even though deep down I wanted to run. He was really here, alive and in the flesh, not on the crossroads. The dread that settled in my chest was worse than anything that I'd ever felt before.

As the Lord of Shadows' pale face emerged from the inky black, I grabbed Papa's hand and pulled him into the wormhole. Before I could take a second step, something wrenched us apart and Papa flew back into the gym.

"No!" I said, snatching myself from the pull of the wormhole. I fell facedown on the gym floor and busted my lip. I was sorry for disobeying Papa again, but I wasn't sorry for staying behind.

The Lord of Shadows hovered in midair supported by hundreds of writhing ribbons. Some of his ribbons had grabbed Papa by his ankle and dangled him upside down like he was a child. Papa clawed at the shadows, but the color was draining from his face fast. The Lord of Shadows was absorbing him, *killing him.*

"Let him go!" I screamed, wiping away tears.

The Lord of Shadows laughed, and his voice quaked through the room like an echo that could shatter glass. His face glowed like moonlight, and his violet eyes glowed too. He was more frightening in real life than he'd been on the crossroads. "You get to watch another one of your children die, *old friend*," he said to Papa. "You should've known that I would find her eventually. You never learn."

"Hey, Brainiac," I yelled at him. "I came into your world, not the other way around. So I guess that means I found you!"

Maybe it wasn't a smart move to taunt an immortal being who could kill gods. But it worked. While his attention was on me, the color stopped draining from Papa's face.

"That was a foolish act on your part, child," the Lord of Shadows said with a smirk. "But I'd expect nothing less from a spawn of Elegguá. So self-righteous. Are you as meddling as he is?" Not waiting for me to answer, he added, "I bet you are. You look like a meddler. Did your father tell you the awful thing that he did to my children . . ."

Someone should've warned me that the Lord of Shadows liked to hear himself talk so much. I needed to figure out a way to use that to my advantage. My portal was still at my back, so if I could free Papa, then we could escape. The Lord of Shadows wouldn't be able to follow us if I collapsed the portal as soon as we entered it.

"When he split the earth," the Lord of Shadows said,

"many darkbringers died. If it wasn't for me they would have been as extinct as the dinosaurs, which by the way died because of the split too. You can't just split worlds. It's the same as tearing something in two and expecting that things will not be changed forever. Even if you stitch the two halves back together, they're not the same as before. He didn't think about the consequences."

As much as I didn't want to listen to the Lord of Shadows, I understood what he meant. It was like when you balled up a piece of paper and then straightened it out again. No amount of smoothing made it like brand-new. A flash of pain crossed Papa's face. He had lived with this guilt for an eternity, but the Lord of Shadows didn't care.

"It was a mistake," I shouted. My whole body shook with anger. "At least he tried to fix it. You're not trying to fix anything. You just want to hurt people."

The Lord of Shadows' ribbons inched toward me, and my father struggled to free himself, but he couldn't. He screamed and roared and used some curse words I'd never heard come out of his mouth. The Lord of Shadows only laughed until my father switched to the language of the celestials. His words trembled in the room and none of it made sense to me, but whatever he'd said annoyed the Lord of Shadows. Papa cried out as the ribbons tightened around him and encased all but his head in a cocoon.

"Noooo!" I screamed as I pointed the staff at the Lord of Shadows. My tears wouldn't stop coming now. "Leave him alone!"

"If you are going to beg for your brat's life, do it in a language she can understand," the Lord of Shadows said, ignoring me. "Let her see how weak you really are."

"Please let my daughter go," Papa pleaded. "This fight is between you and me."

The Lord of Shadows dropped my father to the floor like he was nothing. I didn't run to Papa. That was what the Lord of Shadows expected. Papa rolled on his side and struggled to sit up, but he couldn't. He was too weak.

"I think not," the Lord of Shadows said.

"You really shouldn't have done that," I said under my breath. Heat rose beneath my skin. "You think you're invincible, but no one's invincible. I'm not going to let you keep hurting my father or let you and your army invade my world."

"You no longer amuse me, child," the Lord of Shadows said, his ribbons lashing out at me. I batted them away with the staff, but they kept coming. If they latched on to me, then he'd drain my powers too. I dove and rolled out of the way. At the same time, the light inside me was getting stronger, more powerful, harder to contain. My magic was growing.

"Hey, why do they call you the Lord of Shadows?" I yelled as I ducked behind the bleachers. "Are you afraid of the light because you have bad acne or something? You know you can get cream for that."

"You're as insufferable as your father," he spat. "I'm going to enjoy killing you."

His shadows writhed through the gaps between the bleachers like vines growing up the side of a house. Instead of attacking him, I tapped my staff to the bleachers, and they snapped closed. His scream shook the room as dozens of his ribbons fell off and shriveled up. I ran from behind the bleachers with more ribbons hot on my trail. I conjured metal spikes behind me to slow them down, but it didn't help. They were so close now that I could hear them hissing.

"Your little tricks won't save you," the Lord of Shadows said as another set of his ribbons cut me off. I stopped, my sneakers slipping, and almost lost my balance.

I turned to face him and laughed so loud that for a moment he froze.

"You're not as smart as you think," I said, stepping closer to him.

"Maya, no," Papa said, still trying to get to his feet.

"I bet there is a reason you spent all that time sleeping in the shadow of a star." Something that had puzzled me finally made sense. Every time that I'd seen the Lord of Shadows, he was, well, *in shadows*. What if he couldn't stand the light?

His ribbons crept across the gym, coming at me from every direction. There were no tricks left to play and nowhere to run. I inhaled a deep breath, then let go all the heat and light inside me waiting to burst free. The whole room lit up and the Lord of Shadows recoiled. His writhing ribbons retreated from the light too.

Maya: 1.

Lord of Shadows: a big fat 0.

"Now." Papa grabbed my shoulder from behind. "That won't stop him for long."

And he was right. The Lord of Shadows slinked closer again, and his darkness began to overtake my light.

I wrapped my arm around Papa's waist, and we limped into the wormhole together. This time the walkway inside was chaotic. God symbols flew everywhere. We'd only made it a few steps when the walkway disappeared completely, and we fell hard and fast down a long dark hole.

"Ahhh," I screamed.

"Maya, don't lose your concentration," Papa shouted as we collided into each other. "We can still get through if you focus."

My ears popped, and I couldn't catch my breath, let alone concentrate, but I tried. I didn't focus on slowing our fall because the Lord of Shadows had entered the wormhole too. His ribbons stretched behind us, speeding to catch up. We couldn't let him enter the human world, so I concentrated on closing the portal while we were still inside. Even if it meant trapping Papa and me in the Dark too.

Have you ever heard of the phrase *light at the end of the tunnel*? Well, that was exactly what I saw as we continued to freefall through the wormhole. As we got closer, I could see a bed of yellow and white tulips and sunlight on the other end.

Papa sent flashes of light behind us to slow down the Lord of Shadows. His ribbons drew back but only for an instant. They swallowed the light just as we dropped out of the wormhole. It turned out that I had miscalculated, and the exit was hovering somewhere near the top of a tree. We fell the final few feet and landed hard in the bed of tulips.

There was no time to breathe a sigh of relief, as some of the Lord of Shadows' ribbons shot out of the wormhole, too. The space around the wormhole turned gray, and darkness started to seep into our world. Dread rolled in my belly as I channeled my powers through the staff again, preparing for one last strike. But both of the cranky twins, Miss Ida and Miss Lucille, struck the ribbons with their magic first. The ribbons recoiled back into the Dark, and I had just enough strength to close the wormhole with the staff.

"Maya, you're okay!" Frankie screamed, peering down at me, her face bright.

Tears pricked my eyes again. I couldn't believe it. My friends were alive. Nulan had lied. I shouldn't have ever doubted that Frankie would have a plan.

My voice got all choked up, and I couldn't get a single word out. I sank against the grass, smiling up at the oak tree and the blue sky. There was so much color in our world, and it was all so beautiful.

Eli nudged one of my sneakers with his foot. "I want to know everything that happened after we left."

"Of course you do," I finally said.

"Everything," Frankie added, to be clear.

I laughed.

My friends helped me and Papa to our feet. Papa and I both took in our neighborhood. The colors, the smells, the people. Mama stood with her hands on her hips, sandwiched between the Johnston twins, who looked as cranky as ever.

"Maya Janine Abeola," Mama yelled. "You're in big trouble."

"I know, Mama," I said, ducking my head. "I'm sorry."

Papa leaned against the oak tree. He still looked sick, but he was going to be okay. "She is in trouble, Clarisse." He winked at Mama. "But she did save her old man's life. She should get credit for that."

Mama smiled through the tears sliding down her cheeks and pulled me and Papa into her arms. I let myself collapse against my parents, feeling safe for the first time in weeks.

TWENTY-NINE

GUARDIAN OF THE VEIL

"Dᴵᴰ ʏᴏᴜ ʀᴇᴀʟʟʏ have to land in our tulips, Maya?" Miss Lucille shook her head. "Do you know how hard it is to grow anything?"

"Um, sorry?" I shrugged. "I'll make it up to you."

Papa and I had landed smack in the middle of the twins' flower bed underneath the oak tree in front of their house.

"Give the girl a break." Miss Ida nudged her sister in the side, even if she was scowling at the crushed tulips too. Then she snapped her fingers, and magic that looked like ministars lit up around the tulips. In a split second, the tulips righted themselves and were like brand-new.

Eli smacked his forehead. "Hard to grow, huh?"

Miss Lucille pursed her lips. "Well, it's the principle that counts."

Mama fussed and looked me over for injuries, but aside from the cut on my lip and a few bruises, I was okay. I was more than okay. My friends and I had saved Papa. I couldn't have done it without them. I looked around our neighborhood, taking it all in. The sun was high in the sky, and the birds sang in the trees. My neighbors went about their business as if Papa and I didn't just drop from a wormhole in the sky. I saw the last of the cranky twins' memory-altering magic floating on the wind as a neighbor waved to Papa.

"You're back from your business trip already, Eddy?" Mr. Reese called from across the street. He was sitting on the top step of his front porch working on one of those model ships he liked to build.

Papa waved at our neighbor, flashing a peevish smile. "I hope for a long time this go around."

"Are you sure you're okay?" Mama asked, feeling my forehead for the umpteenth time. Then she pressed two fingers against my wrist to count my pulse. "Your heart rate is a little high. Maybe we should take you to see Dr. Kate for a checkup."

"The young guardian will be fine," came a musical voice from behind me that rang out in the most perfect notes. "Welcome back, Elegguá and Maya."

I turned to see the orisha of beauty, Oshun, in her Miss Mae human form, which was as majestic as her semidivine body. She wore a shimmering gold pantsuit and a choker of black pearls. Her hair was done up in an elaborate crown of jewels that glistened in the sun. How I had never recognized that the owner of our local beauty shop was a goddess was beyond me. Even now she had that extra spark about her.

"The council must speak to you, Elegguá, about these *unfortunate* recent events." Oshun glanced to my friends and me, her expression guarded. We already knew better than anyone what was at stake and the threat still in the Dark.

"Unfortunate events?" I said, my voice tense. I wanted to give her and the orisha council a piece of my mind. I was still mad at them for not trying to save Papa.

Mama cut her eyes at me without even saying a word, and I knew now was not the time.

"We also need to talk about what to do with the children," Oshun said quietly.

"Do what with us?" Frankie nudged up her glasses. "You mean you want to erase our memories like everyone's else's?" She turned to me, her eyebrows knitted together in a thoughtful frown. "Except for our parents, no one outside of the orishas and a few godlings remembers it happening."

"No way I'm letting you near me." Eli backed away from Oshun. "I like my memories unmanipulated, thank you very much."

Miss Lucille rolled her eyes. "If we were going to erase your memories, we would have done it by now."

"What do you mean, then?" I crossed my arms.

This time Mama cut her eyes at Oshun. "I would like an answer to that question as well."

Oshun bowed her head to Mama and smiled. "We will share that information in due time, Clarisse. For now, we must talk to Elegguá *alone*."

Nervous, I looked between Mama and Papa, who exchanged a glance. What did any of this mean? The fight was far from over, but the Lord of Shadows was trapped in the Dark, so we were safe for now. It could only be about the veil, which was still failing.

"I need to get home!" Eli said before jetting off. "I stopped by to check on Jayla when I got back, and she was not happy that I left. Now I need to bake three dozen snickerdoodle cookies to make it up to her."

One of these days I'd have to ask them how they'd gotten to Chicago so fast. The gateway they'd entered led back to Daniel Boone National Forest in Kentucky.

"I'm officially grounded for the first time in my life." Frankie grinned. "Which means I'm stuck in my room doing scientific research. *Such a hardship*."

Once my friends headed home, Miss Ida and Miss Lucille set off for the community center with Oshun and Papa.

Instead of looking Mama in the eye, I stared at my very dusty shoes. "I'm sorry, Mama," I said. "I know I shouldn't have gone into the Dark, but . . ." My voice caught in my throat. There was no excuse, so I bit my tongue and told the truth. "No *but*s. I chose to help Papa, and if I had to do it all over again, I would."

Mama let out a deep breath and wrapped her arm around my shoulders. "I know, Maya," she said, her voice gentler. "I'm still upset, but I understand why you did it. I'm just so thankful the both of you came back safe and sound."

"And now that I'm back, I'll do extra math tutoring to make it up to you," I said when she pulled away and picked grass out of my locs.

Mama shook her head as she looked me over once more. "You're going to need to do a lot more than that this summer to make up for breaking the rules three times."

I bit my lip and rocked on my heels. "I figured as much."

"Come on," she said, her voice heavy and tired. "You need a bath."

I sniffed my armpit and wrinkled my nose. A bath was an understatement. I was pretty sure that I would have to throw these clothes away, they were so dirty. "What will the council do with us?" I asked as we walked up the steps to our greystone. My legs ached, and I felt like I could sleep for a week. It was good to be home.

"I don't know," Mama answered, her face set in a deep frown, "and that worries me."

• • •

The next morning, Papa wanted to make his famous blueberry marmalade, but Mama stopped him in his tracks. His skin was still a little gray, although his color was coming back and he was moving better. Mama cooked breakfast instead for the first time since I could remember. I was tearing through my second batch of bacon and eggs when someone knocked on the front door.

Papa went to answer, and when I heard Miss Lucille's gruff voice, my heart sped up. "The council has made a decision. They would like you, Clarisse, and Maya to come to the community center."

"What's the decision?" Papa asked, his words echoing in the hallway.

"We've been friends for a long time, and you know I'll go to the ends of the universe for you," Miss Lucille said. "But I'm bound by the council's decree, as are you."

Papa grumbled, but he said nothing more.

The walk to the community center with Miss Lucille, Mama, and Papa was somber even though it was beautiful outside. At least the neighborhood was back to normal. My ex-babysitter Lakesha was adding another art piece to her tree collection. This time, an old scratched-up stop sign that she had spray-painted neon blue. We passed some older kids playing basketball on the sidewalk, the snow cone stand, and the elotes cart.

Resident bully Winston rapped to a party of two in the

park. His friends Candace and Tay were the only ones paying him any attention. When we passed by, he glared at me. I guessed I was still on his to-beat-up list. Too bad I couldn't throw it in his face how my friends and I saved his life along with everyone else's.

I went through the metal detector in the community center in a daze and arrived at the golden doors that led to the gods' realm. As soon as we stepped inside, my eyes landed on the bleachers, where Frankie sat with her moms and Eli sat with Jayla. There were other people from our neighborhood here too. The ice cream truck driver, the corner store clerk, and several teachers from school. Principal Ollie in their usual impeccable suit and shiny shoes. No Ms. Vanderbilt, though, which was a relief. If she was an orisha, her powers would be coming up with hard math problems.

The orisha council sat on their thrones in their semi-divine forms.

Shangó (Mr. Jenkins), the orisha of thunder and lightning. Eshu (Ernest), the orisha of balance. Nana, the orisha of the earth. Oshun (Miss Mae), the orisha of beauty. Ogun (Zane), the metal and war orisha, with his six-eyed dog, General, at his feet.

I wondered how many on the bleachers were godlings versus orishas. I remembered what the council had said, so probably not many were godlings. They whispered to one another as we sat down in the empty space left on the front row. I was nervous but squared my shoulders to look brave.

"We have called this meeting to report on the state of the veil," Nana said, silencing the whispers in the room. "As some of you know by now, the veil is failing. We knew that it wouldn't last forever."

"Will there be another war?" someone higher up on the bleachers asked.

"There is no need to jump to conclusions," Oshun said in her musical voice. "But as a precaution, we have called for reinforcements from the celestials who dwell in the sky. They should arrive soon."

"If it's war the Dark wants," Ogun said, sitting forward, his fists clenched, "then it's war we'll give them." General's six eyes grew wider and hungrier, too. "We swore to protect the human world, and that we will."

Ogun's anger sparked more whispers, and Eshu raised a hand to silence the crowd this time. "It's balance that we need, not war."

"How can we have balance if the veil fails?" Frankie's mom, Pamela, asked. "What evidence do you have to support that balance is the answer?"

"I will keep repairing the veil." Papa spoke up. "That's all we can do for now."

"That's why we've called this meeting," Shangó said, lightning sparking across his skin. "Elegguá, you have done this world a service by keeping the veil intact, but there are more tears every day."

Nana leaned forward on her throne, her eyes shimmering. "We ask permission for Maya to become a guardian in training to help protect the veil."

Everyone in the room went quiet again. Scratch that: everyone *except* Eli. He whistled loud enough to ruffle the fireflies lighting the ceiling.

"Yes!" I answered, bouncing on my seat. "I'll do it!"

Mama and Papa narrowed their eyes at me for speaking out of turn. That wiped the smile off my face.

"Your parents must agree to the arrangement," Eshu said. "Elegguá and Clarisse, this is a great responsibility, and we don't blame you if you say no, but we must ask."

Papa looked to Mama, his face worried. It was clear that it was up to her. Mama sat rigid next to me, and I reached for her hand. When she looked down, there were tears in her eyes, but she smiled. "I give my permission," she said to me instead of the council. "But you'll still have math tutoring, and if your grades slip—"

"They won't," I said quickly. "I promise."

"See that they don't," Papa added, then winked at me.

I couldn't stop wiggling in my seat with excitement. This was really happening. My neighbors buzzed with excitement and chatter about the news. Some slapped me on my shoulder and congratulated me. A fresh batch of tears pricked against my eyes. For the first time since my father went missing, these were tears of joy.

"Don't let it go to your head," Eli warned, poking fun. "Your ego is big enough."

Frankie nudged him in the side. "Like you're one to talk, ghost boy."

As Frankie and Eli got into yet another silly argument about nothing, I let out a deep sigh.

From that moment on, I was a guardian of the veil.

Well, technically I was a guardian of the veil in training.

Author's Note

Dear Reader,

I had such an absolute blast writing *Maya and the Rising Dark*. In many ways, Maya and her best friends remind me of my twelve-year-old self: a ghost-hunting science nerd who loved superheroes. I was also an avid reader, but I never saw anyone who looked like me in the fantastical adventures I enjoyed so much. This motivated me to start writing down the stories already percolating in my head.

Along with never seeing myself in books as a kid, I later came to realize that I didn't know much about my own ancestors who'd been enslaved and forced to bury their beliefs and traditions. As I take the journey to recover these traditions, I know that my perspective will be that of a person from the diaspora. I will always have a different way to interact with, process, and understand the traditions of my ancestors. Yet, it's important for me to find my path and connect in some small way through my own stories.

When I first got the idea for *Maya,* I knew two things. First, I wanted to write about a black girl growing up on the South Side of Chicago who loved superheroes. I didn't want to focus solely on the struggles of her neighborhood without celebrating its strong sense of family, friendship, and community.

Second, I wanted to write about discovering the traditions of my ancestors. When I chose to write about the orishas, I did so knowing that I could never speak for anyone raised in the tradition, but I could carve out a little corner for myself and Maya too.

I hope, dear reader, that you experience the joy of discovery that Maya feels as she learns that she is more than meets the eye—that she will become the hero of her own story.

Best,

Rena

ACKNOWLEDGMENTS

I couldn't have written *Maya and the Rising Dark* without the people who have supported me from when this story was only an inkling of an idea to the final draft. I am always most thankful for my mother, who encouraged my love of reading and storytelling. To my brothers, who have been excited about *Maya* since day one.

To Cyril for listening to my incessant talking about Maya and her friends. For your patience and your support during the ups and downs, the good writing days and the bad ones too. For being dedicated to your passion and helping me find balance when I'm so deep in the writing cave that I lose my way.

To my literary agent, Suzie Townsend, thank you for

being an advocate of Maya and her friends from the beginning and working diligently to find this story a home. Thanks to Joanna Volpe, New Leaf Literary Agency's fearless leader and mastermind. To Pouya Shahbazian, the best film agent in the known world and my go-to person for the latest on the best movies. To Mia Roman and Veronica Grijalva for shopping *Maya* in the international markets. To Meredith Barnes for your wealth of advice on publicity. To Dani, who always keeps me on track. To Hilary, Joe, Madhuri, Cassandra, and Kelsey, thank you for your support.

To my thoughtful and sharp-eyed editor, Emilia Rhodes at Houghton Mifflin Harcourt. I count myself lucky that *Maya* ended up in your capable hands. This story has been such an exercise of self-exploration, and I poured so much of myself into this story—thank you for supporting and encouraging me since our very first call. It means so much that I could write this story centered on black kids who aren't that different from how I was as a kid.

I am so lucky to have a great team who supports *Maya* at Houghton Mifflin Harcourt. Thank you, Zoe Del Mar for heading up marketing and Tara Shanahan for publicity. Your work is so key to making sure that people know about the book and getting it into the hands of young readers. To Sharismar Rodriguez and the design team who came up with the amazing cover concept for *Maya*. To Elizabeth Agyemang, Samantha Bertschmann, Mary Magrisso, Kiffin Steurer, Ana Deboo, and Emily Andrukaitis.

Much respect to cover artist, Geneva Bowers. You really brought Maya to life with your beautiful work.

Thanks to these generous authors who read early drafts of the book and offered such kind words: Anne Ursu, Lamar Giles, Stephanie Burgis, and MarcyKate Connolly.

To Mickey Mouse connoisseur, Ronni Davis. Thank you for your energy, kindness, and friendship. It's always fun to talk about stories and characters and a million other things with you.

To my ride-or-die friend and critique partner, Alexis Henderson. Thank you for your unrivaled support and for being my very first reader for *Maya*. Your enthusiasm and early notes were invaluable.

To my #ChiYA family: Samira, Gloria, Lizzie, Ronni (Hi again!), and honorary members Anna and Kat. To Reese, Mia, Lane, Rosaria, and Jeff (who left us for warmer weather), my writing tribe. To the Speculators, who adopted me into their family: David R., Antra, Nikki, Axie, David M., Nikki, Liz, Erin, Alex, Helen, and Amanda.

Thank you to the countless others who have offered me encouragement and support throughout the years.

The biggest thanks to the booksellers and librarians for

championing *Maya and the Rising Dark*. And to the readers who've taken a chance on my words, thank you for your support. Always a big thanks to Mrs. Okeke, my high school AP English teacher, who left us too soon. Her passion made me realize that writing could be more than a hobby.